Crazy about Ava

LILY CLARKE

AIRES PUBLISHING

This novel is entirely a work of fiction. The names, characters and incidents portrayed in it are the work of the author's imagination. Any resemblance to actual persons, living or dead, events or localities is entirely coincidental.

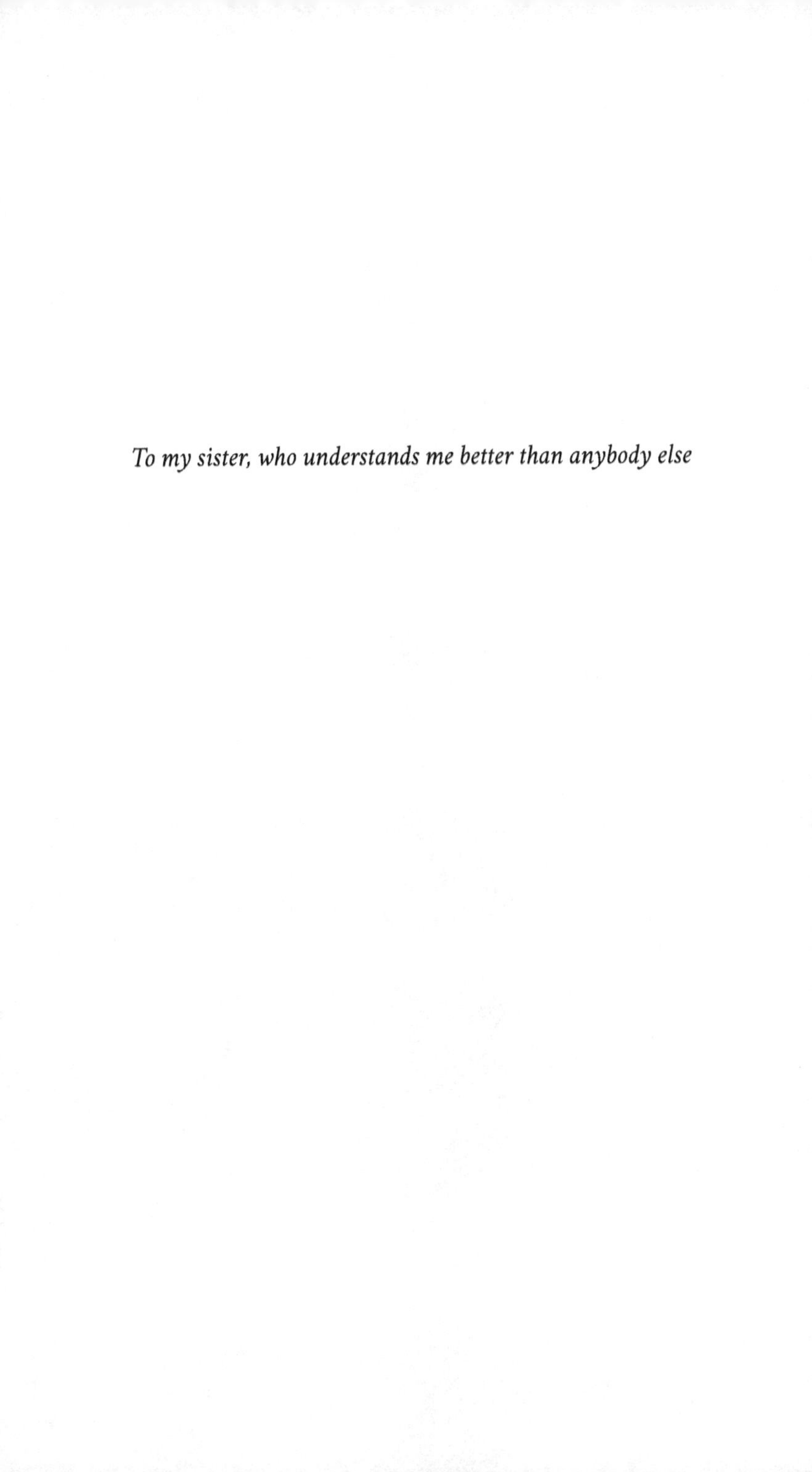

To my sister, who understands me better than anybody else

1 day with Ava

L iam Stewart entered the coffee shop as if he owned it. Considering he could have bought it, expanded it into a billion dollars franchise, and sold it at a hundred times its original value, he could be forgiven for his tendency to arrogance. The coffee shop staff were more than used to his self-assured walking and polite, but demanding, way of ordering. In fact, they were looking forward to his visits. He was the richest man in the area, which seemed to make him a local celebrity. It didn't hurt that he was also ridiculously good-looking. He was tall and lean, with broad shoulders. His hair, a midnight black, was cut short on the sides and longer at the top, where an unruly curl always hung over his forehead, disrupting his otherwise pristine appearance. The fact that he was aware but gave no notice to the attention he generated, went a long way to forgive his abruptness.

That morning, however, he failed to command the immediate assistance of the coffee shop employees. They were gathered around a woman he had never seen before, laughing at something she was saying. She was tall, almost his height, with long brown hair and a fringe that reached to her enormous hazel eyes. He approached the counter and waited to be served. He would have said he was waiting patiently, but his furrowed brow and pursed lips made it clear to anyone looking that he was displeased. It was good that nobody was watching him. He finally coughed loudly. The unknown woman was the only one to notice.

"Oh, my, there's a good-looking man waiting to be served. I think this is my cue to go," she said. The coffee shop staff voiced their upset about this piece of news. She laughed—a loud sound that reverberated in the small shop. "I'll come back and finish my story. This is the best coffee I've had in a while. You have my undying loyalty." She stood up and lifted a large backpack from the floor.

"Excuse us for the delay," one of the staff said to Liam. "I think we were all engrossed with the story."

"Don't worry, Sam, it's fine," he said. He went to retrieve his wallet, but a hand crossed his line of vision before he could move.

"Charge his coffee on my card, Sam," the woman with the backpack said. "It's the least I can do for making him wait."

"There's absolutely no need," Liam said.

"I insist." Sam, the coffee shop clerk, gave her card back with the receipt. Liam tried to hand some cash to the unknown woman.

"Please." Liam turned to her and gave her the look that closed deals, part prince charming, part scary beast. "I don't feel right accepting this coffee for a two-minute wait."

"Now it's done," she replied. "But you can buy me coffee another day, say tomorrow same time?" He stiffened

"I'm engaged."

"Oh, well, I tried. Another day, another rejection." With a wink at Liam, she left the coffee shop.

* * *

LIAM WAS a man of routine or, as his employees liked to put it, anal precision. Not that he'd ever say it to Liam's face. After leaving the coffee shop, he always drove to his office to start the day, but the encounter at the coffee shop had left him strangely off-kilter. He sat down in his car and sipped his coffee, trying to understand why he was feeling like that. If he didn't know better, he'd say she had laughed at him. Nobody had treated him with anything but respect—bordering on fear—for the past five years. A voice coming from the other side of the street interrupted his thoughts.

"Liam," he heard someone shouting his name across the street. His sister Liv was waving at him, four large shopping bags at her feet. "Can you help me with this?" she said. He left the car and crossed the street.

"How did you buy so many things by 9 am?"

"This is all for the wedding. It's the stuff we ordered, it just arrived at the shop. I didn't expect it to be so heavy, though," his sister said. "Can you drive me home?"

"Liv, I need to go to work. I'm already late as it is."

"Oh, ok. I'll take a taxi then. Don't worry." He sighed and grabbed her bags. He lifted them and gave a surprised 'oomph'.

"How did you carry them all the way here? Let's go," he said while crossing the street towards his car.

"No, no, don't worry. I don't want to interfere with your work," Liv said, trailing in high heels after him.

"It's alright, it'll be quick."

"Are you sure?" she said. "I don't want to be the cause you work overtime." He gave her a peck on the cheek.

"I always work overtime and you're never the cause. Hop in. I'll just take my first calls of the day from home." Still reluctant, Liv put the last bag in the rear seat of the car. She opened the passenger door and sat down next to her brother. "By the way, I've left you a new invitees list on your desk this morning," Liam said. "I had my assistant include some more names to it."

"That's fine. Do you want me to send it to the wedding planner?"

"No, I've already done it."

"My brother," she said with a smile, "always so efficient. But please, let's not add any more names. I wanted to do a small thing but the list just keeps growing."

"Don't worry, it'll all be perfectly organized." Liam turned on the engine. He glanced in the side mirror, easing into the morning traffic. " By the way, Scarlett was asking me yesterday when you're going shopping for the bridesmaid dresses."

"Oh, my friend Ava arrives this week. Once she's here, we can all go together."

"Perfect. When does she arrive? Thursday? Friday?"

"Hmm, yes, one of those days." Liam looked at her with his infamous furrowed brow. Liv hunched her shoulders. "She had a few things to do before coming. She gave me an approximate date only," Liv said.

"That's unacceptable. Scarlett has a busy agenda and she cannot plan around your college friend."

"Ava has never failed me. She said she's coming this week and she'll come."

"Tell her to be more specific. That's how things are done. You give a date and time and don't have everyone dancing in attendance to you. You need to call her and demand she confirms the exact day."

"OK, I'll call her when we get home." Liam nodded, satisfied his sister would do so.

* * *

As soon as they got home, with a glance at his watch, Liam tried to take the bags from the trunk, but Liv assured him she could carry the four bags by herself. He protested, but she pushed him towards the house. With a last glance at his watch, he gave up. Liam rushed up the central staircase towards the library, which acted as his study when he was at home. He had a call in two minutes and he didn't want to be late. Liv took the bags to her room, making the walk up the stairs on a couple of trips. Despite the size of the house, they kept very few employees. Or at least they had few compared to their other wealthy friends. They just had a cook, a handyman, and a cleaner, all of them living off site. It surprised most people. They assumed that with that much money, they would live more lavishly, but when they were kids, they had had little money and their parents had taught them the value of doing household chores by themselves. They only kept those three employees because they had been with them since they were children and felt more like part of the family.

* * *

Thanks to the lift, Liv was at home much earlier than expected and she had a few hours free before her next appointment, but before she could decide on what to do next, she heard the doorbell. She frowned; they weren't expecting anyone. Wait a moment. She was expecting someone, even if it wasn't today. It had to be her friend Ava. She rushed downstairs, but Sandra, the cook, had beaten her to the door. The door opened to show Liv had been right.

"Ava!" Liv shouted from the stairs and run towards her friend. She embraced her in a tight hug, which wasn't a simple thing to do as the other woman was carrying a large backpack. "I can't believe you're finally here." Ava hugged her friend back and her laugh resonated in the room. They released each other, but Liv kept a hand on Ava's arm. "Oh, my God, and your hair is so long," Liv said. "I'm so used to seeing you in your pixie cut."

"And I can't believe you're getting married. He must be one smart guy." Liv released her friend and guided her towards the dining room. She asked her to wait for her and went to the kitchen, coming back with two mugs of coffee. She handed Ava a decaf. Her friend didn't consume caffeine. She joked she already had enough energy without adding stimulants. Both friends sat down to drink. There are certain people who it doesn't matter when it was the last time you saw them. You could have met them a week, a year, or a decade ago—it always feels like yesterday. Ava and Liv were one of those. You could hear their voices and laughter coming out of the dining room.

"When will I meet Mason?" Ava asked.

"My brother has organized a party on Thursday," Liv said.

"Why the formality? Drive me to his house this instant."

"You haven't changed one bit, have you? You make everything sound so easy."

"That's because we create most of our problems and I refuse to do that. Anyway, you know I'm cool with anything. On Thursday, we meet Mason at a party organized by your brother; it sounds perfect to me." Ava stood up and paced around the room. Shelves occupied the entirety of one wall, all the way to the ceiling, full of books. The furniture was old fashion, but new, recreating an antique library. Ava spun around, taking it all in.

"Liv, I know your family had money, but I didn't know how much until I saw this house," Ava said. The dining room, where they were, was the size of a ballroom. The dark mahogany dining table could easily accommodate twenty people. She went to the dining-room door and looked out, appreciating the house entrance. It had a wide entry hall with a staircase leading to the second floor. She could see from a half-open door a spacious kitchen, with all white furniture in a shiny finish. Liv crossed her arms and put a hand on her neck.

"I guess it's too much space for just the three of us." She smiled ruefully. "I can't believe in all the time we've known each other you haven't visited before. It's Liam's money, really. He's doing a good job with our parent's company."

"I still remember your stories about him and how he was the coolest guy at any party."

Liv waved a hand in the air as if dispersing Ava's words.

"I'm afraid that's the old Liam. New CEO Liam is all about work and responsibilities. But you'll love him. He's the best." Ava sat down on the couch next to Liv.

"My dear, you're like a sister to me, which makes him my brother. I'm sure we'll get on like a house on fire." Liv's smile faltered. She covered Ava's hands with her own.

"I'm just so happy you're here, and a whole month before the wedding. My brother has prepared a full schedule and I'm counting on you to help me survive it," she laughed.

"I'm happy to see that you, my dear Liv, haven't changed one bit either. That big heart of yours is always too happy to do what you're told. So, what's first in your schedule?"

Liv took out her phone, and Ava laughed when she saw Liv's calendar. It had every single hour of the day accounted for, with different colors and very detailed descriptions of each of the appointments. As Liv read it, an alert popped up informing her she had to be at the dry cleaners in three hours. She rested her chin on her hands and waited for her friend to click on each of the daily appointments and murmur to herself the driving distance between each one. When she was halfway through the day, she looked up.

"Mmm, today I have lunch with the wedding planner to go through the latest details. My brother has sent me an email to read in advance. Would you terribly mind if I take some time to go through it?" Ava waved her hand in the universal gesture of 'don't even ask.' "In the afternoon, we need to pick up my sister Nova and get the presents for Mason's family. His father loves flowers, so we're getting him some flower arrangements. His mum likes… ugh, we'll leave that one to the end. I know nothing about music and Liam is recommending we buy her some concert tickets. I'll wait until he's back to get that one and go by his opinion."

"Tell me, dear Liv, just how involved is your old brother in your decisions?" Liv looked genuinely confused by the question.

"You sound just like Nova. They have arguments about this all the time. I just find it easier to follow his advice. He's always right. He's the one that should complain about all the work we give him, but he's only got one month left to put up with me and then he'll have one less responsibility." Liv went back to her phone to check the rest of her schedule and she missed the expression in Ava's eyes. Ava finished her coffee and left the glass on the table with a loud thump.

"I can't wait to meet him. I'm sure I'll love him."

Liv might be a people pleaser, but she was no fool. She might have missed Ava's eyes, but not the tone of determination in her voice. It was always dangerous when Ava sounded like that. There was a reason people in college called her the steam roller. Nothing came in Ava's way when she had a goal. For a moment, she wondered if by inviting Ava a month early she had started a battle between her friend and her brother she couldn't control.

LIAM HEARD some excited voices coming from downstairs and assumed her sister's friend had arrived. Earlier than announced. He wasn't sure he was going to like this friend of Olivia. However, he felt it would be rude not to say hello and resigned himself to a couple of minutes of awkward introductions. On his way downstairs he saw Thomas, the handyman, lugging a large backpack upstairs and stopped mid-stride. There was something familiar about that backpack, but he was sure none of her sisters had one. Remembering where he had seen it, a shiver run down his spine in dread. He leaped down the last of the stairs and forced the dining-room door wide open. His sister had her back to him and turned at his sudden entrance, but he only had eyes for the woman standing next to her. The same strange woman he had met at the cafe was looking at him in surprise, no doubt in a mirror of his own face.

"LIAM, I was about to get you. I want you to meet my friend Ava," Liv said. "Ava, this is my brother, Liam." Liam entered the room and extended his hand towards Ava. He didn't know exactly what he was expecting, maybe for her to hit on him again, or laugh at him—also again. She just shook his hand and smiled.

"Nice to meet you, Liam. Thanks for letting me stay at your house." He tried to answer, but his voice broke. He coughed twice.

"My pleasure," he finally said.

"What a delightful house you have. You don't see houses with staircases anymore." Was that laughter in her eyes? No, she was being polite. He was reading too much into this. He realized the conversation had continued, and he hadn't paid attention.

"Excuse me?" he said.

"Ava was asking if I'm free tomorrow for lunch, but you

and I agreed to meet with the wedding planner." Liam hesitated. Tomorrow at lunch was his only free time in a week. He wasn't sure he could reschedule.

"Don't worry, Liv. We'll find another time. We have an entire month," Ava said.

"I'm sorry," Liam said to Ava. "I'm quite busy this week."

"I completely understand," she replied. Suddenly, her eyes lit up. "Actually, maybe I can go with Liv to the appointment and we free some of your time."

"That would be fantastic," Liv said, putting her hands together in enthusiasm. Liam was about to interject, but Ava was faster.

"Great. I love it when things have straightforward solutions."

Liv offered to give her friend a tour of the house and show her to her room. With a couple of "see you later", they left. For the second time that day, Liam was left wondering what had happened. Was the plan to exclude him from that appointment? He didn't have any particular interest in organizing Liv's wedding, but his sister cared more about other people's feelings than her own, and he didn't want anyone taking advantage of her good nature. Liv didn't have any reason to exclude him, did she? Liam checked his watch. He had another meeting. He'd have to let this go, at least for now.

As he closed the library door, he remembered Liv's friend laugh. The small hairs on the back of his neck lifted and he consciously run a hand down his neck. He wasn't going to like this woman. Not one bit.

* * *

IT WAS LATE AFTERNOON. Liam came downstairs to find Sandra still in the kitchen. She was usually gone by then. He asked her what had kept her and she replied she was preparing some snacks and leaving for the day. "Snacks for who?" he asked. Growing up, Liam's parents had one rule since they were little: no requests to Sandra that would keep her after hours. Liam and his sisters had tried, of course, but Sandra knew the rule and had always replied that they had two capable hands and could do it themselves. This time, however, Sandra smiled at his questions and, instead of replying, she put a tray in his arms loaded with food and ordered him to take it to the pool. "Did Liv put you up to this?" Sandra laughed while she untied her apron behind her back. She waved goodbye and left Liam standing in the middle of the kitchen with food in his arms. Sandra had prepared olives, hummus, chicken tenders, garlic bread, carrots, and fries. He at least knew this wasn't for Liv, as she hated carrots. He opened the door to the pool and called out to Nova. Instead, a brown head emerged from the water and smiled at the food on the tray.

"I can get used to living here if this is how you treat your guests," Ava said. Liam pursed his lips, debating if he should explain they always treated their guests right or that he wasn't her waiter. He turned it on her.

"Why did you force Sandra to stay past her time just to prepare this?" She looked surprised at the question.

"She offered. We had a friendly chat this afternoon and my stomach made a funny noise. I tried to stop her, but she said she can't leave people hungry," she said.

He harrumphed and placed the tray on a small table by the pool. He made to leave, but she swam to the edge of the pool near him and rested her arms on the border.

"Why don't you join me? The water is perfect."

"In my suit?"

"You can take it off. Don't hesitate on my account." She wiggled her eyebrows and smiled. He straightened his jacket.

"Let's stop this here. I believe I have already told you I have a girlfriend."

"I believe you said fiancé. Does she know she's been demoted? In any case, I have no interest in touching engaged men, but I can certainly look." She kept a straight face, but the humor still seeped through her voice. He looked at her with hard eyes. She sighed. "Fine, I won't look." She covered her face with her hands, but moved her fingers so she could peep at Liam through them.

"I have no interest in skinny dipping at my own house," he said.

"So you do it elsewhere? Interesting… Can I meet your girlfriend and ask her to take some nudes for me?" Ava rested her head on her arms and looked up at him with wide, open eyes. Liam sighed and laughed at the same time. He straightened his jacked again, but stopped mid-motion, conscious of it.

"Have a good time in the pool, Ava."

He opened the kitchen door to get inside. He could hear the water moving behind him. Out of curiosity, he turned to see what would cause so much noise, only to find Ava right behind him. Surprised, he stepped back and collided with the half-opened glass door.

"What are you doing?" he said, his voice a touch too high and his eyes wide. She brought a hand behind her back and moved it towards him. For a second, he thought she was going to touch him. He looked down at her hand and saw that she was holding a bowl of olives.

"Do you want one? It's too much food for me." Liam eyed the olives and, despite his best efforts, he also looked down at her. It was right in his line of vision. She was wearing a pink bikini, worn so often that it had stretched and become loose on her. It wasn't particularly revealing, but it hung on her as if she didn't care whether it sit right or fell off. Liam hesitated.

"Come on, let your hair loose, take an olive. Come for a swim." It was the wrong thing to say because his face closed off and his back became ramrod straight.

"I don't have time to relax. I'm responsible for too many people," he said. Ava took the olives back and popped one in her mouth.

"I'm not sure your sisters and girlfriend will want to hear you call them responsibilities. It's most unromantic."

"I find love always comes with a responsibility towards the other person."

"That I can't argue with." She walked back to the pool and left the olives back on the tray. "However, I always thought it was about sharing responsibilities equitably, and you seem to assume them all. But what do I know? I've never been in love." She flopped onto a deck chair and grabbed a book. Liam remained by the door.

"And what if the other person cannot carry as much responsibility as you can?" he said. "Nobody ever gives in equal measure. You just give what you can and accept the other person." Ava turned on the deck chair to look at him.

"And with that, you almost became perfect. It's a shame you're so bored." He put his hands in his trouser pockets and took a few steps towards her.

"Did you just call me boring?"

"I said you're bored, not quite the same." She turned back on the chair to face the pool and leaned back. She took the carrots and hummus and proceeded to devour them. A shadow blocked the waning afternoon sun. She looked up to find Liam looking down at her.

"Want some hummus?" she said. She extended her arm, and he caught her wrist. He tugged her away from the deck chair and put one arm behind her back and the other underneath her legs. With no visible effort, he took her into his arms. The book she had on her lap landed on the floor with a thud.

"What are you doing?" She laughed and looked wonderingly at him.

"Having some fun, apparently." He grinned and launched her towards the pool, hummus and carrots still in her hands. She landed on her back and gave a tiny yelp before her mouth filled with pool water. She came out still holding the two bowls, one with soaked hummus and the other empty. Carrots floated around her. She laughed, but with her arms incapacitated, she half-submerged again. She sputtered water. He was crouching by the pool, looking at her. One arm rested on his knees.

"Was it fun?" she asked. He shook his head, but his smile reached his ears. She narrowed her eyes, not believing him for a second. Slowly, a half-smile showed on her face and she swam towards him. He backed away from the pool, never losing sight of her, reading her intentions.

"This suit costs thousands of dollars."

"I'll pay the dry cleaner," she said. He shook again his head and retreated into the house. From the kitchen, he looked from the window to see her swimming on her back surrounded by carrots.

"Do you mind if we stop by Liam's office? I need to drop this."

Ava and Liv had spent a good couple of hours with the wedding planner going through the music set list. Apparently, that was one of the few things that Mason wanted to be involved and his taste and Liam were a bit different. A lot different, actually. Two hours hadn't been enough to find a balance between the two men's suggestions, but the wedding planner had to run to another appointment. Ava didn't blame her. At some point, Ava proposed ditching all suggestions and for Liv to start her own playlist. In Ava's opinion, the wedding planner had looked hopeful, but Liv said she looked scared. They'd never know who was right because Liv refused to ignore her fiancé's and brother's ideas.

Liam's office was more unassuming than Ava expected. Based on Liam's demeanor and fashion taste, she was expecting slick, state-of-the-art facilities. The reality was much different. It was an old brick building, nestled between a flower shop and a dry cleaner, in the old town. The interior looked like a set from the 80s, with a flashy carpet with geometric forms, and yellowish light fixtures. At reception, there was only an old lady who was answering phones as if she had three pairs of hands and four ears. When she saw Liv, she came out from behind the reception desk and hugged her. She was very short and came around Liv's shoulders, but she gripped the younger woman with the strength of a weight lifter. Liv returned the hug and asked her questions about her health and her family. In the background, the phone kept ringing, but the receptionist ignored it completely. Liv's parents had hired the receptionist when she was in her twenties. She knew Liv and her siblings since the time they were born and she regaled Ava with some stories about Liv's childhood.

The same scenario kept repeating itself with every person they found on their way to Liam's office. It warmed Ava's heart to see it. It felt like one big family.

By the time they arrived at Liam's office, it had been over thirty minutes from the moment they had stepped into the building. Liv looked at Ava sheepishly, but her cheeks had a cute rosy color and her eyes were shining. Ava couldn't stop smiling either. Liv knocked on the office door and opened it. Liam was behind his desk, talking to another man. He looked about the same age as Liam and was wearing a suit, but whereas Liam was tailored and wrinkle-free, his looked like it had been passed down from his father—or grandfather. He was as tall as Liam, but dedicated less time to exercise, and his figure wasn't as trimmed. When he saw Liv, he rushed to his feet and stammered a shy hello. Liv gave him a hug and a kiss on the cheek. He blushed, but Liv didn't notice as she was already walking towards Liam. When she had greeted him too, she introduced Ava to the unknown man. 'Meet Will,' she said.

His hand was massive compared to Ava's, like a bear holding a phone. He was warm, in a pleasant type of way.

While Liv updated Liam on the playlist situation, Ava and Will chatted quietly by the door.

"Have you been working here long?" Ava asked.

"About five years—since Liam took over—but we've been friends since school."

"Oh my, and you were willing to work for a friend? I don't know if I'd risk the friendship," Ava said.

"Not at all. He's the best boss you can have. He's patient, values others' opinions, and doesn't micromanage. I trust he'll always be fair."

"I didn't expect that answer," Ava admitted. "He certainly doesn't give that impression."

Will rubbed the back of his neck and glanced at his friend.

"He can come across as overbearing sometimes, but he gets hundreds of people asking him to make decisions for them every day. So many people expect him now to tell him what to do, that he just does it automatically, I guess. But I've met no one that can listen to the way he can."

"I might ask you to remind him that someday," she said.

He chuckled and turned to look at his friend.

"I know what you mean," he said.

Liv kissed his brother goodbye and joined them.

"It was nice to see you again, Will, but we need to rush to pick up Nova. You never come over anymore. We miss you. Liam," she said, turning to her brother, "make sure you invite him home more often."

"Th—thanks," Will stammered. "I don't want to be a bother." She touched his arm, and he gulped. Liv didn't notice.

"We're always happy to see you."

Ava couldn't help smiling at their interaction. She looked at Liam and saw a matching smile on his face. Liam glanced at Ava, and their eyes connected. She covered her mouth to avoid bursting into laughter. He bit his lip and dropped his head, ruffling some papers with no purpose. He looked up again and exchanged a nod with Ava.

* * *

LIV PARKED the car in front of the bus station. Both she and Liv left the car. Suddenly, a blur passed in front of Ava and enveloped Liv as the facehugger from Alien.

"Sis," the facehugger said. "Can I leave my suitcases with you? I got this call from some friends and I'm meeting with them now, but I'll get home later this afternoon." She released Liv enough to let her breathe.

"Sure, but first let me introduce you to my friend Ava." After what she had seen, Ava decided that Liv's sister wouldn't mind if to get a hug. Ava was a hugger, and it made her happy when she found another one. She put her arms around Liv's sister and squeezed. She was squeezed back with equal force.

"I'm Nova," Liv's sister said. "I have so many questions to ask you. Liv told me about your job and I just can't wait to hear how you manage it."

While Nova and Ava were chatting, Liv looked behind her sister and noticed a pile of luggage behind her. There were three large suitcases, one backpack, three large plastic bags, and a box. She frowned.

"Nova, is all that yours?" Nova stopped what she was saying and looked behind her towards where Liv was pointing. She looked at her sister, but quickly averted her gaze.

"Yeah, it's all mine."

"Why did you bring all that? Did they kick you out of the dorm or something?" Nova bit her lip and played with the zipper on her hoodie.

"Something like that," she said. Her eyes moved between Ava and Liv, only to move away from them both. She took a deep breath. "I'm not going back to college after your wedding." Liv opened her eyes wide. She opened her mouth to speak, but Nova looked at her watch and cursed. "I really need to go, sis, but I'll tell you about it later, OK? Nice meeting you, Ava. See you both later." She was walking backward as she spoke, waving at them. A car pulled next to her and lowered the window. A head appeared through the window and called Nova's name. She jumped in surprise, smiling when she recognized a friend of hers. With a last wave at Liv and Nova, she opened the car door and disappeared inside.

Liv and Ava were standing in the parking lot, looking at the retreating car. When it left the station, they turned their attention towards Nova's possessions. Ava tilted her head.

"I don't think it will all fit in your trunk," she said. Liv puffed her cheeks and released her breath slowly.

"Liam is going to kill her."

* * *

AVA HAD DISCOVERED a cozy little nook in the library. Well, it was a library, but it also functioned as Liam's home office, evening living room, and just a place to hide away. Ava loved it. It was warm and lived in. She hated showroom houses. It's not that Liv's house looked fake, but it had a clear divide between the top and bottom floor. The ground floor was for guests. It had the majestic dining room and the slick kitchen. There was a pool and a garden that was well taken care of. It was a house that spoke of money and prestige. The top floor, however, was a family home. Here it was where they really got together and relaxed. And out of all the rooms, the library was the best one—in Ava's opinion, at least. By the time the Stewarts spent here, it was theirs too.

That day Ava had a couple of hours to herself. She had

found a book that she had been wanting to read for a while and, after making sure Liam didn't need to use it for work, she had set herself up for hours of uninterrupted bliss. She had considered bringing some snacks too, but she didn't want to dirty the space.

The sun was disappearing when she heard some loud voices coming from downstairs. She could distinguish Liam's voice, resonating deeply through the doors. She wasn't sure who was the other person at first, but they seemed to be getting closer to the library, and the voice was sounding clearer. It was Nova, her tone deeper than Liv's. She heard a couple of steps and Nova's voice got really sharp. She must have been standing right outside the door. Liam's steps followed. She could now hear the conversation as if they were in the room with her.

"It's my money," Nova was saying.

"I won't let you waste it," he shouted back.

"That's not your decision to make. "

"It is until you're twenty-five. You're going to finish university and get some actual work experience first. You'll then realize how foolish your idea is."

"How dare you?" she roared.

"You have no life experience."

"Because you won't allow me." Silence followed. Liam spoke again, but he was more subdued.

"Please, Nova, listen to me."

"Why should I when you don't listen to me?" she replied. "What do you know, anyway? You never started a company. Mum and dad did that for you. You don't want to give me MY money? Fine, I'll do it without it and without your help." Nova's shoes click-clacked on the floor as she left until the sound faded away completely.

"Nova," Liam shouted. "Nova!"

* * *

THE DOOR OPENED and Liam stormed in. He was murmuring something about stubborn people and messing his hair, pacing up and down the door, only to stop short when he spotted Ava by the window.

"It's rude to eavesdrop," he growled.

"In this case, it was also unavoidable," she replied, closing her book. "You have a very commanding voice. And you're also very firm. You modulate it in the right places to empathize your points. Do you have stage training? Your employees must feel intimidated by you."

"I don't shout at my employees," he replied.

"Interesting…" She opened her book again and continued reading.

Liam left the room, only to come back a few seconds later. He was patting his pockets and looking around the room, clearly avoiding the spot where Ava was sitting.

"Are you looking for this?" Ava was holding a phone in her hand. Liam thanked her as he took his mobile from her extended hand. He left the room again and Ava returned to her book, but one more time he came back in.

"I only want what's best for her," he said from the door. Ava only smiled and nodded. "She has no clue how hard it is. The pressure and the stress." He hesitated. "I rarely shout at people."

"I'll admit that my experience with families is limited and, perhaps, not the best, but I understand that it's common between siblings to fight, especially when they are at different points in life," Ava replied.

"She could lose all her money," he said. "I almost lost all mine and our parent's company with it. I don't want her to experience the agony I felt."

"And she probably knows that." He crossed his arms.

"You disapprove of my approach," he said. "But you don't know the whole situation."

"You're probably right. Please, don't mind me. I'll pretend I heard nothing."

"Where is Liv? I thought you'd be with her."

"Waxing. We're best friends, but I don't think she needs me there."

He nodded once, a faint color rising to his cheeks. He clasped his hands behind his back and looked around the room. Ava returned to her book, but he just stood there.

"Do you need me to leave?" she asked.

"What? No, no," Liam walked over to a bookcase and retrieved the closest book he could get. He tugged it under his arm and waved goodbye to Ava. He stopped mid-step.

"Why is your experience in families limited?" he asked suddenly. He looked surprised he had even asked. Before Ava could reply, he apologized for the question and left the room.

He was already far away when she replied, her voice uncharacteristically low. "Because I had no one like you in my family."

3 days with Ava

The party organized on Thursday with Liv's fiancé was actually dinner at La bonne chance, one of the fanciest, swankiest, and most expensive restaurants in town. Liam didn't believe in being fashionably late, but Nova was of a different opinion, which is why, when Ava was ready, she found him at the top of the stairs shouting at Nova to not test his patience. Liam was pleasantly surprised to see that Ava was ready one minute before. She was wearing a simple but elegant black dress. None of the Stewart siblings would ever admit it, but they all wondered what sort of clothes were inside Ava's ratty backpack. To Liv's surprise, when she saw her unpacking, she pulled out gowns, cocktail dresses, and fancy clothes that didn't even need ironing. Liv joined them and they waited for Nova, who, oblivious to Liam's constant yells, took her time to get ready.

* * *

THEY ARRIVED at the restaurant fifteen minutes late and with a dark cloud over Liam's head. He hated being late. He had actually spent all the ride to the restaurant reminding Nova of that fact. Ava watched in amusement how Liv tuned them out and she guessed this was a normal occurrence. Even with the delay, they were the first ones to arrive, which did nothing to improve the older brother's mood.

"People are busy," he muttered. Nova and Liv both ignored him.

"Well, clearly, otherwise they wouldn't be late," Ava replied, misunderstanding him on purpose. He scowled at her, but couldn't say anything else because the first guests had arrived.

* * *

AVA KNEW IMMEDIATELY who Mason was by the way Liv's face lit up. She also knew that Liam didn't like him one bit by the way he greeted him. She had seen people picking up dog poo with more enthusiasm than the handshake between brother and fiancé. Mason was big, taller than anybody else in their small group, with blond locks and a firm square jaw. He looked like a posh Viking. Liv introduced Ava, and Mason greeted her with an exaggerated bow.

"A friend of Liv's is my friend," he said. Liv giggled and playfully batted his arm.

"Stop it, you're always such a fool."

"Only for you, babes, only for you," he replied as he grabbed her by the waist and gave her a kiss. Ava could tell her friend was completely infatuated. He was certainly easy on the eye with his broad back and luscious blond hair, but Ava couldn't fully trust someone that used the word 'babes'. She knew it was an unfounded prejudice, but nothing in her experience had helped her dispel it. She was hoping Mason would be the one to do it that night.

The rest of the members of the party were Mason's best

men: Mark, Moses, and Mike. They were all friends from college and apparently called themselves 4M. Ava laughed dutifully at the poor joke.

La bonne chance was, as its name suggested, a French restaurant. Why all fancy wedding dinners happen at French restaurants it's anybody's guess. Regardless of the cliche, the food was indeed delicious, and the company was pleasant. Nova and Ava, both of a chatty disposition, carried most of the conversation, and there was enough wine to make the 4M happy. Not that it took much to make them happy. They were young and wealthy men without a care in the world. Even Liam seemed to relax with a glass of wine in one hand and the other draped along the back of Nova's chair. Right after the main course, Nova's phone rang, and she stepped out to take it.

Liam had booked the table for most of the night. It allowed them to keep having drinks well after the food was over, which in hindsight, Liam would admit, wasn't a very smart decision. Nobody had told him that Mason was a singer. A drunk singer. He stood up and opened his arms wide.

"Ladies and gentlemen of this fine establishment," he shouted for everyone to hear. The dining room conversations quieted and everyone looked at him. Even some waiters stopped with plates in their hands. "In four weeks, I'm going to marry this woman. Aren't I lucky?" The whole restaurant clapped and congratulated them. "But," he continued, "she's also lucky, aren't you, babes?" Liv was blushing, smiling, and hiding her face behind a napkin all at once. "She's lucky because," and he paused dramatically, "she gets this for the rest of her life." This was the moment when he improvised a rap song about Liv. The audience was divided about the quality of the singing, or lyrics, or performance in general, but Liv was staring at him as if he was the sun.

* * *

"SO YOU AGREE WITH ME," Ava heard Liam say behind her. Mark, the former occupant of the chair next to Ava, was standing and dancing to Mason's rap and Liam had occupied his chair. Liam leaned over and put an arm around Ava's chair so he could talk quietly with her. "That's he's a complete moron," Liam clarified. "I can see it in your face. You're laughing at him, not with him."

"That's a fine distinction you're reading in my face."

"But I'm not wrong, am I?" Ava moved in her chair to look at him.

"You're preparing a very grand wedding for someone you hate so much."

"This is for Liv, not for him. Maybe if I give them a good start..."

"You know that's not how it works, right?" she said, and he shrugged.

"What else can I do? She won't listen to me."

"Are you asking me for advice?" she asked. He looked taken aback by the question. "Pity," she said because you'd find it useful."

"Let me guess, you'll give it to me, regardless."

"Of course not. I never give unwanted advice." And she said nothing else. Liam should have been pleased, but he suspected she had given him that unwanted advice, nonetheless. A final clap interrupted his thoughts. Mason had decided to have mercy on his ears and finished his little act. And just in time, because the maitre d' didn't look any happier with the performance than Liam did. Liam ordered some more drinks and a round of water, hoping the hefty bill he was going to pay that night would compensate for Mason's lack of talent. He looked at his sister one more time, laughing at Mason's antics, and hoped he was wrong and that Mason would make her happy.

Mark came back to his seat, but Liam waved him away. Ava looked him in the eye and smiled. He grunted.

"If I'm going to survive tonight, I can't seat any longer next to his friends. And Nova still hasn't come back. She must have run away, clever girl."

"And here I thought it was because you wanted my company," she replied. Liam smiled and said nothing. He realized they were standing too close and moved back, but he didn't take his arm from her chair. Mason started to use the table and glasses as percussion instruments, and Ava tapped her foot in sync with him.

"You're not enjoying this," he half asked.

"Maybe I enjoy being in proximity with you," she said. He huffed a laugh.

"Will you stop that? I know you don't mean it."

"I can't. Your reactions are too funny. You look so discomfited by my comments." He rubbed his face with his free hand, thinking about what she just said.

"Maybe it's because nobody has spoken to me like that since I took over the company. You have zero respect for my position."

"I cannot see how a job position determines a person's respect. But do you hate it so much? Do you feel insulted? Because I don't think I can stop. It's so much fun to see you blush." He stopped rubbing his face and looked into her eyes.

"Maybe I like it too much." She studied his expression before laughing out loud.

"Oh my, we might still make a real boy out of you."

At that moment, Nova returned to the table and sat down next to them both, interrupting their conversation. She grabbed a fork and took some leftover food from Liam's plate. "What did I miss?" she asked. Liam shushed her. "If he knows you missed it, he might start again," he said.

* * *

IF SOMEONE HAD ASKED LIV, she'd have said that the night was being a success. Mason and his friends were definitely having a good time, Ava was chatting with everyone, and Liam… Liam didn't look too miserable. She knew that her brother didn't think her fiancé was good enough for her. He had never hidden his opinion on the matter. In a discussion, Liv always tried to understand the other person's perspective and she could see why Liam might dislike Mason, but he failed to see her perspective. Mason offered Liv something. She wouldn't call it a way out because she wasn't miserable in her current life, but it was a step forward in a moment where she felt like there were no clear steps.

* * *

THE FIRST TIME that Liv met Mason, she had thought him handsome. More than handsome, actually. Mason was built like a Greek sculpture. She didn't mind one bit when he approached her at the bar. And when he had talked to her, he said something that nobody had said to Liv before—he called her smart. It wasn't that Liv thought she was stupid, but in a family of overachievers, she had always been called kind, or pretty, or nice. She was never the smart one. Hearing Mason calling her that, she had felt special. With Mason, she didn't feel inferior—quite the opposite; she admitted to herself that one time. She felt needed. He needed her. Especially when he got into one of his 'prank moods', as his parents called them. "He isn't a bad person," they'd say. "He just doesn't really know when a joke goes too far." What they always failed to say is the type of pranks he had pulled over the years, some including paying hefty fines or pleading in front of the judge. One time, they expelled him from a school when he took pictures of the director's naked butt and pasted photocopies of it all around the school. Another time, he thought it would be grand to change his extremely religious uncle's Christmas tree baubles for dildos. He posted online the video of the family's reaction when they found it on Christmas morning.

There were usually three situations that could cause his prank moods: lots of alcohol, someone he wanted to impress—that was mostly his friends, although on occasions Liv was enough—or being bored. So far, Liv had prevented Mason from doing any prank in front of Liam, but as she saw Mason drinking more and more at the restaurant, her face lost a bit of color. When her brother raised his arm and asked for the bill, she gave a sigh of relief.

* * *

THEY LEFT the restaurant at midnight. The night air was pleasant and it matched their mood. Ava closed her eyes and smelled the Spring air. All of them had drunk and Liam had asked the restaurant manager to call some taxis for them. "They're five minutes away," Liam told them. At that moment, Mason tried to cross the street and Liv was grabbing his arm to hold him back. He tried to get away, but Liv didn't let him go. Liam went over to check what was the problem.

"He wants to drive," Liv said. She crossed her arms and faced away from Mason.

"I can't leave my car parked here. Someone might steal it," Mason said. He got loose and jumped onto the road, but Liam and Mike, one of his friends, held him tight.

Ava looked across the road to check his car. She couldn't

really help herself. Cars always fascinated her. The moment she saw it, she knew which one was Mason's car. It was a monstrosity in yellow, one of those sports cars that announced a middle life crisis or an extremely small... appendage. Ava also knew that it was a massively inefficient car, which in her books meant it was a piece of trash, no matter how much Mason had paid for it. She must have been staring with her mouth open because Mason saw her and stopped trying to cross the street. Instead, he stumbled over to her. She could smell his breath. Someone should find him a glass of water.

"It's a beauty, isn't it?" He had misinterpreted Ava's expression. "A total chick magnet, too."

'Ugh,' Ava thought, but she didn't say it. "It certainly makes a statement." What kind of statement she better not say out loud. Mason was satisfied with her reply. He told her how much he had paid for it, how fast it was, and how often he washed it.

"Definitely a piece of trash," Ava thought. Except she must have said it, because Mason recoiled. "I mean the cars next to yours," she amended. Ava never found out if he had believed her because the taxis had arrived. Mason's friends helped Liv get Mason into one of the taxis. Liam offered to go with her in case she needed to carry Mason into his house, but his friend Moses lived nearby. Nova, Ava, and Liam piled into the last taxi and headed home. At the last minute, Liv got out of her taxi and waved at them to wait. She got in with them.

"He's staying the night at Moses," she said as an explanation for the switch, and everyone pretended to believe it. "Liam, next time, less booze, please. I feel like my head is spinning." Liam replied something, but it was so low that they couldn't hear it. Perhaps it was for the best.

* * *

LATER THAT NIGHT, Liv accompanied Ava to her room. She flopped onto her bed as Ava got ready to sleep.

"So, what do you think of Mason?" Liv asked from Ava's bed.

"You didn't tell me he looked like that," Ava replied and Liv laughed.

"He's so dreamy, isn't he?"

"Are you marrying him for his body?"

"Of course not. He's great," Liv replied. When Ava didn't reply, Liv jumped from the bed. "You don't believe me? You don't like him." Ava plugged her phone into the charger.

"Liv, my dear, you know I don't have the best opinion about families. I don't have any interest in getting married and even less at this age, but that's me. I can see you have a massive crush on him."

Liv laid down on the bed with a sigh.

"I know he's very corny when he sings for me in front of everyone, but I confess I like it. I feel… seen. Liam is the big leader, and Nova has the big personality. I'm the boring one, but with him, I'm not that boring." Ava was hanging her dress after changing into her pajamas.

"My dear, I wouldn't be your friend if you were boring, but something tells me you won't believe me. If he makes you feel that special, then he must be special indeed."

"Do you like him?" There was an eagerness in Liv's eyes that Ava couldn't ignore.

"Is it important to you that I like him?"

"Liam doesn't."

"Then let's do something. Let's ask Mason to join us in the wedding schedule," Ava suggested. Liv visibly hesitated.

"He's not very good at this kind of stuff."

"Who cares? I just want to get to know him better. He's your future husband. Think about it; you'll have him making you laugh while you go through all those boring chores."

"OK, I'll talk to him." And if Liv looked less than thrilled at the prospect of having Mason with them, Ava chose to ignore it.

* * *

LATER THAT NIGHT, alone in bed, Ava was staring at the ceiling of her room. It's not that she had trouble sleeping—she never had—but she liked thinking in bed. The stillness of the night helped her clarify her thoughts. Ava knew from experience that all families were fucked up. Admittedly, some more than others, but they all had their struggles. What she didn't see that often was the love she could see in Liv's family. Most people would have found this sad, but Ava didn't have anyone to tell her how wrong she was, so she just took her experience as the measure of truth. However, despite the obvious love between the siblings, from what she could see, they didn't talk to each other. Liam gave orders, Nova was rebelling, and Liv—she had to do something about Liv. Any other person might observe this and decide to leave them to sort it out themselves, but Ava couldn't do that—Ava was a fixer. Some people she had encountered in the past used other words like meddlesome or bossy, but if she had listened to those people, she wouldn't have fixed their problem, would she? However you'd like to call it, Ava hated seeing problems unsolved, being those problems the secret of electric cars or dysfunctional families. She had almost a month left in Liv's house and she was determined that by the end of her stay, Liv and her whole family would be truly happy.

* * *

LIAM WOKE UP WITH A START. He listened into the night, looking for a noise that could have woken him up, but everything was quiet. He couldn't remember what he had been dreaming, but he could tell it was pleasant. What could have woken him up then?

The next day, Liam drove Liv and Ava to his favorite coffee shop. He was meeting Scarlett, his fiancé, for breakfast. Going into the coffee shop with Ava made him recall the first time they met in that very same place. He looked sideways at her, but she seemed unperturbed. It bothered him. Liam was a good-looking man. He'd had women coming onto him all the time. He shouldn't feel awkward in this situation. If anything, she should be the self-conscious one. But she wasn't. How annoying. He tried to cover his discomfort with excessive confidence. In four strides, he was at the counter and ordering for everyone. He saw Ava approaching from the corner of his right eye.

"Oh, you know how I take my coffee," she said. He blushed like a stupid schoolboy. Before he could make a cutting reply, Sam, the coffee shop staff, passed him his card back.

"Have a nice day, Mr. Stewart."

"They call you Mister?" Ava asked.

"They are being polite," he replied.

"Or they think you're older." He looked at her and there it

was again, that edge of mirth in her eyes. Surprisingly, he laughed.

"Yeah, because I've got my shit together. I don't traipse around with a dirty backpack." She pursed her mouth, acknowledging the hit.

"Someone knows how to have fun, who knew?" Ava said, and Liam lifted an eyebrow.

"So this is your idea of fun, huh? I think I get you now."

Scarlett chose this moment to come in. She was tall, with raven black hair cut in a fancy bob, all straight lines and shiny. She smoothed out the wrinkle that always appear in between Liam's brows and kissed him lightly. Liam introduced her to Ava, who jumped straight into a hug. The four of them moved to the side of the counter to wait for their drinks. Ava was full of questions for Scarlett and the two of them were chatting animatedly before their drinks even arrived.

That was something Liv always envied about her friend, how she could talk to anyone and anywhere. She always felt too shy with strangers.

They were caught up in the conversation when a stranger approached them.

"I can't believe it. Ava Ortiz is here. The evil mastermind in the flesh." A man hugged Ava and lifted her in the air. No small feat, considering how tall she was. Ava laughed. "I'm very disappointed with you," he said as he put her back on the floor. "I thought by now you'd have achieved world domination."

"World domination! The actual conquering would be all fun and games, but imagine the bureaucracy involved in the management of it."

Liam and Liv observed this interaction with interest. Well, Liv was watching with interest. Liam seemed annoyed by the loud display of affection. Scarlett looked scared.

"Hey, mastermind, aren't you going to introduce me to your friends?"

Ava made the proper introductions and her friend, Phil, shook all their hands, but he kept Scarlett's hand at the end. He smiled widely at her.

"I've always had a thing for brunettes." He winked at her. Scarlett took away her hand as if he had burned her. Liam wasn't a jealous guy, but his locked jaw said he wasn't thrilled right at that moment. Phil noticed it and pointed at him.

"That your boyfriend?" he asked Scarlett.

"Fiancé," she replied.

"So no ring yet."

Ava got in between them and pushed Phil away.

"Enough of your wickedness." She tooted at him in disapproval. She turned to Scarlett and Liam. "Ignore him. He just likes to stir the pot."

Liv had observed the whole interaction biting her nails. She didn't like conflict and never knew how to deal with it. She was debating what to do when Sam, from the coffee shop, called her name and she rushed to grab her coffee. When she rejoined the group, Ava was still apart with Phil, and both Liam and Scarlett were stone-cold silent and looking uncomfortable and miserable in equal measure.

"Shall we go?" Liv asked, a small wobble in her voice. Both agreed and they left the coffee shop. Liv and Scarlett sipped their coffees and made small talk while they waited for Ava to join them. Liam rested on his car and didn't open his mouth.

* * *

INSIDE THE COFFEE SHOP, Ava whispered angrily to Phil.

"Was that necessary? Surely you could tell they were together."

"It was just a joke."

"If the other party doesn't laugh, it's not a joke. It's being an asshole." She left, ignoring his calls, saying he was sorry. Phil had exceptional qualities as a friend. Behind his flippant attitude, he was actually very thoughtful and caring. He had helped her through some tough times during her teenage years. When it came to women, though, it was like a different person took over. Ava had sometimes problems marrying both sides of his personality and wondered how someone could behave so differently with a woman just because they wanted to bed her.

Before she could leave the cafe, Phil blocked her exit.

"Don't leave like that, please."

"I don't like you when you're like this." He laughed without humor.

"I don't like myself either. I don't know what came over me, OK?"

"What are you doing here? You never answered." He rubbed his neck.

"It's hard to explain. I'm looking for something I lost."

"What is it?" He walked around her before replying.

"Let's call it love." She rolled her eyes.

"Call me when you're back to your normal self. I can't deal with you when you're like this."

* * *

BY THE TIME she joined her friends, Liv and Scarlett had almost finished their coffee. Liam's laid abandoned and cold on the hood of the car.

"Sorry about that," she said to all of them.

"Not your fault," Scarlett replied with a small smile. Despite her kind words, Ava could tell she was looking pale. She was going to kill Phil. He was always pushing people's buttons, but the way he had unsettled Liam and Scarlett was out of all proportion. Liam got in the driving seat and the rest joined him. He dropped Ava and Liv at home before driving Scarlett to her house. Before they left, Ava leaned on Liam's window, but she spoke to Scarlett.

"Sorry about my friend again. What he did was uncalled for."

"Not a big deal, Ava, truly," Scarlett said.

Ava grabbed Liam's hand and squeezed it. He looked up and nodded once before driving away.

5 days with Ava

"Long or short?" Liv asked.

"Short." "Long". Ava and Scarlett said at the same time. Liv grimaced. It was going to be hard to find a bridesmaid dress that suited them both. Ava and Scarlett had very different styles. Scarlett was all about neutral tones and tailored shapes. Ava was more eclectic, moving from bell bottom trousers from the 70s to grunge shirts from the 90s. Ava and Scarlett looked each other up and down, noticing Liv comparing them. They realized what had Liv so worried.

"Hey, don't stress," said Scarlett. "We'll wear anything."

"Yes," Ava added. "Why don't we walk around the shop and see what you like?" She grabbed Liv's arm and interlaced it with her. They went through the racks, checking some dresses and commenting on them. Liv looked a bit overwhelmed.

"Let's start with the color," Scarlett said.

"Mmmm, the flowers have some lavender undertones. How do you feel about something in similar shades?"

Scarlett's dress that day was a light lilac and complimented her porcelain skin perfectly. There was no doubt she would look great in similar colors. Ava, with caramel skin, might not. Liv was feeling like pulling her hair out.

"I love lavender," Ava replied. Liv wasn't sure if she believed it. She didn't put it past Ava to wear a dress she hated to make her happy. Before she could question her, they had reached the section in those colors, and Ava and Scarlett were comparing some they liked. They pulled out six different options and Scarlett went into the changing room to try the first one.

"Where is Nova?" Ava asked.

"She said she had something urgent to do for her business. She's coming a bit later, but she said she's easy, anything will do for her. Nova looks amazing whatever she wears, anyway."

"Building a business will keep you busy," Ava agreed.

"By the way, how come you can take so much time off?"

Before Ava could reply, Scarlett came out of the dressing room with the first pick. It was a long halter top in a light color. With her short hair, it looked stunning on her. Ava and Liv both gave the thumbs up.

Ava came out with the second pick. This one was a shorter version. It was also a winner.

The third one looked great on them, too.

And the fourth, and the fifth, and the sixth.

Liv groaned.

"Can you stop pulling off every single style? You're making this harder." Ava put an elbow on Scarlett's shoulder and moved the other hand up and down.

"When you're working with these two," pointing at their bodies, "it's hard to fail." Scarlett laughed, a nerdy nasal sound coming out. Ava looked at Scarlett. "I'm available to rock this body at your wedding, too. Bridesmaid for hire. The only thing I request is a list of all the cute available men at the wedding."

"Is that how you keep in shape?" Scarlett asked her, waggling her eyebrows.

"With the blood of young men at the peak of their vitality? Yes, it's an old family recipe. My grandmother reached hundred years old with that method."

Ava continued making jokes while they tried the six dresses again side by side. Each time, they discarded one until they had only two left. By that time, Nova had arrived too. She tried on the two finalists until they chose the one. Liv and Nova went to place the order and pay while Scarlett and Ava waited for them sitting by the door. Scarlett was laughing so hard that she started to complain that her stomach was hurting.

"I haven't laughed this much in so long," she said.

"Well, this is one of my talents," Ava replied.

"Making people laugh?"

"That makes it sound so pedestrian. I remind them how to be young." Scarlett's mouth quirked to the side.

"We sometimes need that reminder, don't we?" There was a hint of sadness in her voice. "I never thought I'd need that reminder at twenty-nine." She said it so low that she doubted anybody had heard.

* * *

WHEN THEY HAD ALL the dresses sorted out, the four of them went to grab a drink.

"To Liv's upcoming nuptials," Nova said. They clinked their glasses and drank. Scarlett leaned forward and gestured for them to get closer.

"So, is it time for some dirty details about Mason?" she whispered.

"What do you want to know?" Liv asked with a sly smile.

"How does he place amongst all the guys you've been with?" Nova asked. Liv pretended to gasp in shock.

"Little sis!" She then crossed her legs and grinned. "He's right at the top. Right. At. The. Top." They all giggled.

"I knew you were marrying him for his body," Ava interjected. Liv denied it loudly.

"No, no," Scarlett said, waving her arms up in the air. "He cannot be the top one and the husband." She had already had some champagne at the bridal shop and the cocktail was making her tipsy. Not that the others were sober themselves. "There will always be two key men in your life: the one that makes you see the back of your head and the one you marry. Confess, there was someone else that placed higher than Mason." Liv hid her face in her hands and nodded. They all rushed to ask who it was, but she just shook her head and mimicked sealing her lips.

"Scarlett," Nova said, "we need to hear some embarrassing stories about Liam that we can use against him."

"Well, I don't know about embarrassing. It's not like your brother doesn't know his way around the bed." Nova covered her ears with her hands. Liv laughed as she drank and had to cover her nose, liquid almost coming out of her nostrils.

"I take it back. I take it back," Nova said. "I don't want to hear about Liam."

LIV AND SCARLETT were queuing for the toilet. Ava and Nova were doing their best to finish the jug of mojito before the new one arrived. Nova put their two glasses side by side and was pouring in tiny increments to distribute them equally. She passed Ava her glass, and they both relaxed in their chairs.

"Liv is moving out of the house in a month. I can't wrap

my head around it," Nova said. She crossed her arms and took a sip of her drink. "It's been the three of us for so long now. I'll miss her. The house will feel so empty."

"But soon Scarlett will move in. And who knows? You might be an aunt soon." Nova rubbed her lips, thinking. Ava tilted her head, looking at Nova, who realized that she hadn't replied to the question. She dropped her hand in her lap and smiled sheepishly at Ava.

"I can't picture it. Maybe it's because they never talk about it, and Scarlett rarely stays over. It's like while Liv is rushing into marriage, Liam and Scarlett have forgotten about it." Nova shrugged. "Maybe there's something wrong with my family." The waiter came with the new pitcher. He put it on the table and cleared the empty one. Ava refilled Nova's glass.

"Changes are scary," Ava said, "but they're generally for the best. Your family is growing, you won't be alone."

"Don't get me wrong, I love Scarlett, but..." Right at that moment, Liv and Scarlett came back to the table. Nova closed her mouth and smiled at both of them. Ava lifted the jug and poured them both some of the newly arrived mojitos. They all made to drink, but Ava stopped them. She stood up and raised her glass. The rest raised theirs in response.

"To Liv and a life of toe-curling nights." The rest cheered, but when they made to drink, she stopped them. She wasn't finished. "To Nova, to the success of her company." Ava pointed her glass towards her and moved finally to Scarlett. "And to Scarlett, hoping Liam can climb to the top."

"And what about you, Ava?" Liv asked.

"Me? I told you. Give me many young and unattached—preferably hot and witty—men. I hope you point at some of them next week at the party. I need to find some distractions."

She found many things at that party indeed.

Liv knew her fiancé well. She could almost say that not even his parents knew him as she did. But maybe that would be taking things a bit too far. For better or for worse, Mason was a simple man. He liked music; he liked his friends; he liked silly jokes and attention, and—Liv knew this—he liked her. She knew who she was marrying and, at a time when everything seemed confused and complicated, Mason was refreshingly easy. She knew her brother didn't think he was enough for her, but he was good enough for what she needed. If he sometimes was childish, she could handle it. Or at least that's what she thought until the day he came with her to finalize the wedding favors.

Liv didn't know that so many things could look like penises, boobs, or anything remotely related to sex. Mason was showing her that day just how much she didn't know. It was quite simple, really. If it was long, Mason would put it in his crotch, bonus points if it could swing around. If it was round, it was clearly a boob. Anything with a strange shape could act as a butt plug, according to Mason. Liv's cheeks were burning. She couldn't look the shop owner in the eyes, which was making having a conversation really difficult. Making a decision was proving impossible. She recognized Mason's mood: he was bored, and that was never a good thing. When Mason was feeling like that, he came up with the most ridiculous ideas to have fun. They were never fun for anyone but him and his friends. Normally, Liv would try to distract him, but she couldn't do that today and pick the wedding favors. She was becoming stressed. She was about to do the unthinkable and shout at Mason to shut up. Maybe she was thinking of including some swear words in between, too. Ava, however, acted first.

"I'm going to get some coffee, guys. Mason, will you help me bring them all?"

"I'm good, thanks," he replied. "No coffee for me."

"Great, then you can grab mine and Liv's by yourself, right?" she handed him some money. "Mine must be decaf. For Liv, order her usual." He looked confused, either at the money in his hand or because Ava expected him to know how Liv took her coffee. Ava chose to interpret it in a way that suited her. "She takes it with milk, large, two sugars." She patted him on the back and opened the shop door. Still frowning and looking at his hand, he left to get some coffee.

Liv wanted to thank Ava, but she didn't think it would be appropriate. He was her fiancé, after all, and he deserved her loyalty. Ava stood next to Liv on the counter and grabbed one of the favors that Liv had ordered. It was a small fabric pouch with two hands embroidered outside. Inside it had a cotton filling and some sort of tiny balls.

"This is pretty," she said. She turned it in different ways. "What is it?" Liv took it from her and put it back on the counter.

"If you open it there are some seeds inside. They represent growth and... It doesn't matter." Liv put her elbows on the counter and buried her face in her hands. "Why can't I make a decision?" Ava grabbed the favor again and opened the pouch. Some seeds spilled into her hand.

"Maybe you can customize them. You've always been good at handcrafts."

"That would look too… pedestrian. They won't be elegant enough for the wedding."

"According to who? By your last year at university, you were making hundreds of dollars selling your jewelry on campus. It was a legit business, Liv."

Liv fidgeted with one of the favors.

"That wasn't a business. It was a hobby."

"Which is how most business-related to handcrafts start. It was a small business, yes, but it was a business." Liv dropped the favor back on the counter.

"Well, never mind," Liv said. "I just need to choose from these, not add more options." Ava looked at her friend. Liv was biting her bottom lip and was burying her head in her hands, almost bent over the counter. Ava called the clerk.

"Excuse me," she said. "I'm afraid we're not finding what we're looking for." She took out her card and handed it to her. "Please, charge here all the costs so far, but we won't be ordering any more items." Liv tried to get the card from her, but Ava pushed her hand away. The clerk looked hesitant between the two women, but in the end, Ava won.

"What are you doing?" she whispered when the clerk left with the card.

"Show me," Ava said.

"Show you what?"

"Whatever you had in mind for the wedding favors. One of your creations. Come on, I'm sure you even have a picture on your phone." In a rush, Liv moved her bag behind her, worrying Ava might try to get her phone from it. Ava's eyes softened, and she extended an open palm towards her friend. "Liv, they're good enough. They were always beautiful and creative, just like you." Liv bit her lip, which was looking a bit swollen by now, and put a hand in her bag, but she didn't take her phone out.

"I would need to make over a hundred. It's too much work."

"I'll help you. Do you need supplies, or do you have enough at home?" The clerk came back and gave Ava her card back. Ava opened the door, but Liv hesitated by the counter. Finally, she took a deep breath and left the shop. Ava followed her. They were walking towards the car when Liv stopped Ava with a hand on her arm, right in the middle of the street, and showed her a picture on the phone. She was biting her left thumb and one of her feet was taping insistently. Ava smiled and took the phone. She used two fingers to zoom in.

"Liv," she said, looking up at her friend, "these are perfect."

Ava was handing back Liv's phone when it rang. They both leaned forward to stare at the screen.

"Oh, we forgot about Mason," Liv said.

* * *

LIV WASN'T sure how it had happened, but they had ended up in a club downtown that night. When they finished buying some supplies to do the wedding favors herself, it was already time for dinner and they decided to stay out. When they finished eating, someone—she doesn't remember who—said that it was too early to go home. Before she knew it, they were queuing to get into a club. She wasn't dressed for it. None of them were. They wore faded jeans and trainers, and she was pretty sure that the club had a dress code. However, Ava spoke to the bouncer. They seemed to know each other, except Liv knew Ava had never been to this place before because she had mentioned it in the queue. But Ava, being Ava, had befriended him in the space of less than a minute. The bouncer tilted back his head and roared a laugh. They had let them pass. And now they were inside the club and it was hot and noisy and Liv wasn't sure she liked it. She seemed to be the only one, though. Ava and Mason had already ordered some drinks, and they passed Liv a gin and tonic.

They dance and they drank. Mason was doing his silly moves, and Ava was loving them. Was it because she had never seen someone dancing like that? Liv didn't think it was that funny. Mason's idea of dancing involved copying other people's moves behind their backs and making space on the floor to do his break dance routine. Why was Ava still laughing? Why wasn't Liv? She didn't want to see Mason dancing anymore. And she definitely didn't want to see Ava laughing at his moves, either. They weren't funny; they were offensive to the people he copied. Liv went to get another drink, but when she reached the bar, she couldn't decide what to have. She didn't want to drink. She didn't want to be there with his best friend and his fiancé. Why didn't she want to be there?

* * *

LIV WAS STANDING by the bar, an empty glass in her hand, lips pulled down. Ava was on the dance floor, dancing with a good-looking guy. Near her was Mason, lost in his own world, dancing like he didn't have a care in the world. Which he didn't. Ava saw her friend and went to get her. She grabbed Liv's hand and pulled her onto the dance floor. Liv followed her, but she didn't look like she was having a good time. She was barely moving, just swaying in place and looking around the club with pursed lips.

"What's wrong?" Ava spoke close to Liv's ear to be heard

over the music. Liv shook her head and turned her back on Ava as she continued dancing. Ava touched her shoulder to get her attention. She looked at Liv with a frown and a question in her eyes. Liv shook her head again, but Ava wasn't about to be deterred. She took her friend away from the noise and asked her again what was the problem. Liv crossed her arms and leaned against the wall.

"I—I'm just tired. Do you mind if I go home?" Ava didn't mind, of course. "I'll go get Mason," Liv said. "I'm staying at his house tonight. Shall I help you get a taxi?"

"I'll stay longer," she said with a smile.

Liv wasn't sure why she'd had such a terrible time at the club. Ava had been working hard to make sure everyone had fun. She had been trying to get to know Mason well, which Liv appreciated, but she just wished… She wished Ava didn't encourage Mason so much. All the attention Ava had given him tonight had surfaced the worst in him. But Liv didn't want to be unfair to Ava; she didn't know Mason would respond like that. Although she never tried to stop him, either. Liv was talking to herself in circles. She rubbed her temples. If she didn't leave soon, she was going to get a headache. She searched for Mason and found him trying to get onto one platform with a group of girls from a hen party. They were all smiling at him—he was gorgeous after all—and he was soaking all the attention like a dry tissue. When he saw Liv, he moved his arms, inviting her up. She shook her head and asked him to come down instead. He put a hand up and mouthed "in a moment". He wanted to finish that song. Liv waited for him at the edge of the platform. She could see Ava on the dance floor, dancing again with the good-looking guy. Ava was watching her from the corner of her eye. When she saw Liv looking, she waved. Liv waved back and then crossed her arms. Tired of waiting, Liv called a cab and went back home without Mason.

A little before 6 am Ava arrived at the house. She took off her shoes to avoid making noise and waking up the family. Ava thought everyone was still asleep, but as she neared her room, she heard noises coming from Liam's room. She tiptoed to it and found the door half-open. She saw Liam was already awake and opened the door wider.

Liam was doing some burpees and didn't hear Ava. He was wearing shorts and a sleeveless shirt. He must have been working out for some time, as his skin glistened with sweat and his hair was plastered to his face. His phone vibrated, marking the end of the repetition set, and he tapped the screen to reset the timer. Ava leaned on the doorframe and observed him. She was tired, but not so much that she'd miss the view. She bit her lip, trying to contain her laughter at her thoughts.

Liam turned around and saw her. He looked confused as to why she was standing there, but then he took note that she was wearing the same clothes as the day before.

"Someone had fun last night," he said. The timer on his

watch was already counting down, so he stopped it. He grabbed a towel and wiped his face.

"Was it you? I'm so happy for you. Did you remember to untie Scarlett from your bed?" she replied.

"Scarlett is at her house."

"Who's tied to your bed, then?"

"Nobody is tied to my bed!"

"Oh, I thought you said you had fun," she said, her smile wider than usual.

"Is that your idea of fun?"

"Are you asking to tie me up? Oh, my, what will Scarlett say? I've never thought about it, but I'm always up for—"

"Stop it before someone hears you," he hissed.

"You want to keep it a secret, I see," she winked at him. He rubbed his nose bridge with two fingers and put the towel on his left shoulder.

"Why do you always misconstrue my words? What if I did to you what you do to me?"

"Disarm me? Your dimples do that every time you smile. Well, at least that one time you smiled, I found them disarming."

"My dimples—" He stopped himself and took a deep breath. "Just don't let my sisters see you come back like that. I don't want them getting ideas." He picked up some weights, only to put them back down. He seemed to have given up on his workout and was putting everything back in place.

"Ideas about what? What exactly have I done you found so objectionable?"

"Don't you need to go to sleep? I bet you haven't slept at all tonight."

"Why should that bother you?"

"It bothers me because..." He stopped mid-sentence, his arms on his hips. He dropped his eyes, unable to look at her.

"Forgive me," he said. "I have no right to tell you what to do or not do."

"Unless you tie me to your bed, of course," she replied. He couldn't help himself and he chuckled. Ava waved goodbye and left him to get ready for the day. She passed Liv's and Nova's room carefully and grabbed the handle to her door. She moved it in slow motion to avoid noises when a hand stopped her. Liam was at her back, one arm around her to grab the door handle, their hands touching. Ava turned her head to the side to look at him, her back pressed against his front. She could see the sweat glistening on his face. He said nothing and just studied her face. She had spent all the night out and her eyes were slightly red, but she was wide awake. She could feel his body tense, as if he was going to move, but not away from her. At the last moment, he seemed to realize how close he was and let go of the door. He took a couple of steps back.

"I—I want to apologize. I sometimes say what I don't mean when I'm angry. There's obviously nothing reprehensible about spending a night out." She flipped her hair back and her lips quirked up.

"That's because you don't know half of the things I did yesterday," she replied. He was left alone outside her door, shaking his head and smiling.

* * *

LIAM CAME BACK HOME EARLY that day. Through the entrance, he saw the door to the dining room half opened and both his sisters leaning over the table, their arms and hands busy with something. He came in, but both of them were focused on what they were doing and didn't hear him. He peaked over their shoulders at the table. It was full of ribbons, beads, strings, and other materials. "What's that?" he asked. His two sisters stopped, their hands mid-motion. Liv was holding a large needle, using it to pass a black thread through a cerulean bead. Nova was cutting some ribbon. They looked at each other and then back at him.

"We're making some necklaces," Nova said. Liv was still staring at him. He grabbed one from the table. They were delicate silver chains with white porcelain medallions with initials engraved in blue.

"You did this, Liv?" Years ago, before their parents passed away, she used to do a lot of her own jewelry and he recognized her style. "They're good."

"Thank you," Liv replied hesitantly. He turned the medallion around and saw an inscription. *"Liv x Mason, 5 May"*. He took a few more. They all had the same inscription. He looked at Liv and lifted an eyebrow.

"I thought you had ordered some wedding favors already."

"Y—Yes, but I thought this would be more personal." Her voice was thin, and she was looking a little pale.

"You thought so, huh? I find the timing suspicious." He threw the necklaces on the table and clenched his jaw. "You're trying to cover for her, but this has Ava written all over it. I can't wait until this wedding is over and we can return to some resemblance of peace."

Nova raised her chin and finished wrapping a necklace in a small purple bag.

"You only say that because you cannot boss her around. I actually think it's a good thing for you."

"For me? Look at all the extra work she had you doing. I could wring her neck! She's lucky she's not here right now. I don't want to see her face." His voice had increased in volume as he spoke. A slow smile appeared on Nova's face, like a cat about to catch her prey.

"That's funny, brother, because you always seem to gravitate to whatever room she's in." With that parting shot, Nova scurried away before her brother collected himself enough to reply to her. Liv was playing with a half made necklace. Liam dropped the necklace on the table and put his hands in his pockets.

"You shouldn't let Ava convince you to do all this, Liv. You already had the wedding favors. How many hours have you spent doing this?"

"It wasn't her idea." She kept playing with the necklace. "I —I actually wanted to do this from the beginning, but I was afraid it wasn't fancy enough for the wedding." She looked up at her brother tentatively. His face registered the shock he felt.

"I had no idea," he said, his voice back to a normal volume. He grabbed one of the finished purple bags and turned it around in his hand. "These are... The necklaces are great, Liv. You always had a touch for these things." She gave him a small smile and tucked a hair behind her ear. "Do you need help now that Nova has run away?" Liv fidgeted with the string in her hand until it was a messy ball. She bit her lip, put the string down, and took a purple bag.

"We put them inside these bags," she explained to him, "and label them with these, so everyone gets their initials." He grabbed the first bag with surprisingly delicate fingers and tied it slowly and with care. Liv watched him work with a fond smile and a bit of wonder. Nova returned and poked her head through the door. When she saw her brother helping Liv, she gave him a hug from behind.

"You're going to mess this bow," he said. She kissed him on the head and sat down to help, too. After an hour, Nova went to ask Sandra if dinner was ready.

"And what is your friend doing that she's not helping you?" Liam asked. His voice sounded irritated again.

"She helped me for hours this morning, but later she had

a work thing. No, wait, it was something with her family lawyer. No, not the family one, but definitely a lawyer."

"Mmm, I see. By the way," he said, trying to sound casual. "Ava said something about families and unsatisfactory experiences. What was that about?"

"God, what a sad story. I don't think I should tell it, though. It's her personal life," she said as she put another necklace on the table. She stopped, pondering something, and turned to her brother. "I sometimes forget to thank you for what you did for Nova and me when mum and dad passed away. The way you took care of everything, of us. Few people would have done that." Liam's gaze softened.

"No need to thank me, sis. I only am what I am because I had you two with me. I'm only sorry I didn't do better." He closed another bag and carefully tied another bow. He held the bag in front of his eyes, assessing his work. Satisfied it looked good, he carefully put it in the box with all the other presents. He grabbed a new necklace and put it next to the empty bags to choose the best color combination. Liv stared at him the whole time. She sighed contentedly. She scooped her chair up next to his and hugged him. He patted her arm and continued wrapping necklaces while she hung from him for a few seconds. She kissed him on the cheek and returned to her work.

* * *

AT THE BACK of his mind, Liam kept wondering what Liv's reference to Ava's own family meant and how he could find out more.

8 days with Ava

Ava was surprised when she answered the door to the Stewart's house and found her friend Phil. She hadn't told him where she was staying or the address, but he didn't look one bit surprised to find her there.

"Mastermind, you never call anymore. Have you forgotten about me?" He stepped into the house and gave her a big hug.

"How could I?" she said, returning the hug. "I thought you'd be gone by now, but something is obviously keeping you here." He ignored her veiled question.

"Are you on your own?" he said as he looked around the massive entrance.

"I think Sandra, the cook, is in the kitchen. Why? Anything important to tell me?" He shrugged.

"I just wanted to talk to you."

Ava and Phil had been friends since school when both of them run constantly into problems because of their fast mouths. Mostly, it was Phil running into problems and Ava talking him out of them. He enjoyed provoking people, and he sometimes took it too far. However, he had proved to be a steadfast friend to Ava. When she was fifteen and her family problems started, she stayed at his family's house for a full month and he had accompanied her to all the family lawyer's appointments. If he sometimes rubbed people the wrong way, Ava always remembered the other side of his personality that not everyone got to see.

"How's your search going? Did you find the love you were looking for?" she asked. She poured a glass of lemonade and passed it to him. He thanked her and sat down on the library sofa.

"I've found it a while ago," he replied. "The question is how to recover it."

"Are you planning a bank robbery?"

"No, something even more dangerous." A small smile played on his lips. Ava took a sip of her lemonade and sat down next to him. She knew he was being cryptic and dramatic on purpose and she refused to play his game.

"Oh, well, good luck then. Call me if you survive." He laughed and she smiled back at him.

"Nobody gets me like you do, mastermind." He put an arm around her shoulders and leaned his head on hers.

"Which is why I know that there's something you're not telling me, which means it's something bad. Come on, Phil, you know I won't judge you." He didn't say anything for the longest time.

"How do you know if something is a bad thing or not? Say, if you know something will make you happy, how far will you push to get it?"

Ava drummed her fingers on her glass.

"That's a difficult one," she said. "I guess my limit is other people's happiness. If I destroy their happiness to get mine, I'm not sure I'd do it."

"What about your parents?" She sighed and rested further on his arms.

"Did you come to give me a headache?" she asked. He ruffled her hair.

"I came to get the unvarnished truth from you. I can always count on you to be honest with me."

"I can always count on you to put people on the spot." There was no heat on her reply. "I understand why my parents did what they did," she continued. "Maybe what I said earlier it's not right, or at least not entirely. You cannot be miserable just to make someone happy, the same way that you cannot make someone miserable just to be happy. How far can you push for your own happiness you ask? Mmmm, I guess it's a balance and it's up to you to decide what's acceptable. However, maybe—and I'm not saying this applies to you since I don't know the case—if it's that difficult and complicated it won't make you as happy as you believe it will. Maybe walking away will make you happier in the long run. If you really want to know my opinion, though, I'd say that happiness doesn't depend on one single thing. You are not going to be happy if, say, you're doing well at work but your personal life is in shambles. In the same way, you might have the most amazing friends and partner, but if work is painful, you won't be happy. And normally that one thing we obsess about the most as a key to our happiness, it's actually not the one."

"Why am I not surprised that when it's about love you tell me to walk away?"

"What does that mean?"

"It means, mastermind, that even someone as brave and dauntless as you have a limit." He rubbed her arm with the hand he had draped around her. "What if I walked away, though, thinking it was for the best only to discover it wasn't?"

"Why did you walk away in the first place?"

He groaned and looked up at the ceiling.

"Life is too complicated, I don't like it. I don't want to think anymore. Let's marry and have kids."

They heard a cough coming from the doorway. Liam was looking at them from the doorway, two deep grooves between his eyes.

"Am I interrupting?" he asked.

Phil disentangled himself from Ava and stood up to greet Liam. They shook hands. Liam adjusted his suit jacket and it almost looked like he was wiping his hand. He stayed by the door and didn't come into the room.

"I hope you don't mind me visiting your home," Phil said. He was at his most enchanting, when he wanted people to like him. He had the most beautiful smile, with cute dimples showing on both sides. It made him look young and innocent. Liam's face was as rigid as marble. "Ava and I had some catching up to do. We haven't seen each other in a while," Phil added.

"Of course," Liam replied frostily.

Phil noticed the reluctance in Liam's voice and decided it was time to leave. Ava accompanied him to the door, and they promised to call on each other before leaving town. Ava grabbed his arm and squeezed it, making him promise to tell her if he needed someone to talk to.

When Ava returned to the library, Liam was sitting on the sofa reading from his tablet. Ava ignored him and sat at her reading nook to pick up where she left off that morning.

"Is that guy a close friend?" Liam asked. Ava lifted her eyes from the book.

"Yeah, we've been friends all our lives." Liam gave a short grunt and tapped on his tablet screen. Ava could almost hear his thoughts swirling around his head. A couple of times it looked like he was going to say something, but never did.

"Is he staying long in town?" he finally settled for.

"I don't know. Maybe next time keep looking at him as if he were a bug you want to squash and he'll leave in terror."

"I did not look at him like that. I don't know him."

"You were rude to him and you know it."

Liam excused himself saying he had a phone call to make. However, he came back briefly after leaving.

"I'll apologize to him next time I see him," he said to Ava. She smiled.

"I doubt you'll see him again, to be honest."

"God, I hope so," he said to himself.

* * *

SANDRA FINISHED PUTTING the last plate on the dining table and bade the family goodbye. Tonight they had Mason dining with them, Ava had invited him. Liv was sitting down already, waiting alone for the rest. She poured some wine, a large glass. She tipped the glass to drink but stopped halfway. She was suddenly feeling tired and didn't want to play the host. Interestingly enough, in her mind, she was playing the host for Mason, not Ava, although technically it was the other way around.

Ava's reasons to invite Mason so often were reasonable enough. After the wedding, she would leave again and she wanted to get to know him better, but Liv couldn't help feeling that there was something else at play. She shut down that line of thinking before she'd get upset. One by one, the rest of the family joined until Mason, the last one to arrive, sat down.

She was about to take a sip of her wine when Mason stood up, stole the glass from her, and took a big gulp. He then put the glass on the table, made Liv stand up, and grabbing her by the waist, gave her a deep kiss Hollywood style. He laughed and Ava made an 'aww' sound. None of the siblings did. Liam poured another glass of wine and handed it to Liv. Mason sat back down, a smug smile on his face.

"Steak, my favorite," he said. "I hope it's good. I'm a man that knows his meat. You know what I mean?" He wiggled his eyebrows in Liam's direction, hoping the only other guy at the table would join him in the joke, but Liam was pouring a glass for Ava and didn't reply.

Everyone looked uncomfortable except for Mason and Ava. Mason because he had no clue what was going on, and Ava... she was smiling as if that was the most perfect dinner in the world. Liv noticed and narrowed her eyes, wondering again what her friend was plotting.

Ava started then to ask questions to Mason, from the most simple ones like his favorite color to his most embarrassing moment.

"Oh, boy, I have so many of those," he replied. He then told them stories of nights out with his friends. They were those stories where drunk groups of friends do the most absurd things, things not even a toddler would think of trying, but they don't feel any embarrassment about them afterward. Mason actually felt proud.

"And then Mark..." he had to stop because he was laughing so hard he couldn't speak. "He then..." there was another bout of laughter. Most of Mason's stories ended with some nudity, waking up with strangers, or waking up naked with strangers.

"You had some wild years," Ava said. He puffed up his chest unconsciously.

"Yeah, but you know, my mother kept pestering me to give her grandchildren and I guess it's time, isn't it, Liv?"

"How romantic," Nova murmured into her glass. At this point Liam was busy checking his phone, Nova was on her third glass of wine and Liv looked like she would fall asleep on the chair.

"Well," Mason replied, unaware of the sarcasm in Nova's words, "you women like your sweet words, don't you? You're like a full-time job, let me tell you. Don't you agree, pal?" He elbowed Liam.

"I definitely don't," Liam replied. He refused to look at Mason. He put down his phone, cut the steak on his plate, and put a small bite in his mouth, chewing slowly.

"If one day I become as boring as this guy, please someone shoot me." He pointed at Liam and rolled his eyes.

"Deal," Nova replied. Liam tried to hide a smile by taking another bite. When Mason looked at her, she tried to cover it by saying, "Meat, pass me some more meat, please." Liv scowled at her sister, but Mason laughed it off. One good thing you could say about him is how oblivious he was about other people's opinions of him.

"Mason," Ava interrupted. "I heard you are into music."

That was one topic that Mason truly felt passionate about. He lit up like a Christmas tree. He listed all his favorite artists and what he thought were their strong suits. Everyone at the table had to admit that he knew his stuff. He followed the local scene and had spoken to most of them.

"I almost got signed in," he admitted. He had a faint blush on his cheeks and lowered his eyes in an almost self-deprecating manner. 'This,' Ava thought, 'is how he got Liv.' And she wasn't wrong. Liv had spent almost the entire dinner trying to make Mason shut up, but at that moment she was resting her head on her left hand. Her body turned towards him. She had a small smile on her face, tender.

"What happened?" Ava asked. He shrugged.

"I thought I was the shit, you know? I tried to call the shots and compose, sing and produce the album, but the record label wasn't interested in the direction I was taking. When they said that, I told them it was that or nothing, and here I am, eating dinner at my future in-laws." He laughed, but a shadow passed over his eyes. Liv noticed it. She sat down properly again and readjusted the cutlery next to her plate.

"Maybe you should become a music promoter. You know all the local places and can represent promising artists," Ava suggested. Liam and Nova nodded their heads in agreement. Mason wiped his face and put the napkin back on his lap. He seemed to think about it, and they all looked at him expectantly. Except for Liv. She had interlaced her fingers and rested her chin on them, her gaze staring at nothing. Mason shrugged again.

"Too much work." He laughed, a true deep rumble from his belly.

* * *

BY THE TIME they finished dinner, it was already midnight. Liv and Mason had already closed the door to her room. Nova was gathering plates, but Liam told her to go to bed. 'I'll do it myself,' he said. She kissed him goodnight and yawned on her way upstairs.

Liam was stacking plates in the dishwasher. The soft clink they made as he loaded them was the only sound. Soft steps sounded behind him and he knew without looking back that it was Ava.

"Any more surprise guests tonight? Maybe someone nicer this time, like a psychopath?"

Ava left some glasses on the counter next to the dishwasher and started passing them to Liam.

"If you had some sense, you'd have invited Mason to dine at home every day since you met him."

"I already know more about him than I care for."

"You're deliberately missing my point."

He paused briefly before grabbing another glass from her.

"And you criticized me for telling her what to do?" he said.

"I'm not telling her what to do."

"Who's missing the point now?" She laughed, her usual sound reverberating louder in the stillness of the night.

"I want her to be happy," Ava said. "I don't want to leave here without having done everything I can to ensure it."

He straightened his back and closed the dishwasher door. He pressed the start button, and the water rushed into the machine, disrupting the silence.

"I can understand that," he replied. "But I'd appreciate it if you do it in a way that doesn't make me spend so much time with him." She laughed again. He thought about how unique her laugh was, how it always filled the space. It didn't matter whatever noises there were around—dishwasher, cars, other people—he always felt her laugh vibrating through his bones.

"But then I kill two birds with one stone. What can I say? I like to torture you."

"That I don't doubt. Maybe I should torture you back. What would it require?" She tapped her finger on her chin, eyes looking up.

"Make me drive his car?" she replied. And this time, his laugh joined hers. Liam grabbed a kitchen towel to wipe the table, but she stopped him and told him to go to bed. He had an early start for work and she was on holiday. She could finish cleaning. He protested—she was their guest, after all— but she didn't give in. As he left, he could hear her humming as she cleaned. Liam realized that since her arrival, there hadn't been a moment of silence in the house. He should have hated it. Yep, he should have.

9 days with Ava

Liv was preparing a coffee when Liam poked his head into the kitchen. He had an uncharacteristically mischievous grin on his face. A business partner had given him four tickets to a show downtown, and he wanted to ask Liv and Nova if they wanted to go with him. Liv agreed, but she couldn't understand why he had such a glint in his eyes when he said it. Cryptically, he just told her to wear something fancy. "Oh, and tell Ava to come if she wants," he added as he was leaving. Nova tried to pry more into what he had planned, but he didn't give an inch. A couple of hours later, both sisters and Ava were waiting in the living room for Liam. The sisters were wearing short dresses; Nova's was bright red, paired with black Doc Martin boots, while Liv's was all covered in sequins with thigh-high boots. Ava was wearing a short black jumpsuit with a very low neckline and black stilettos. Liv and Nova couldn't stop talking about where Liam was taking them. This was definitely not in the wedding schedule he had prepared and it was very out of character for him. At least, it was for New Liam. The Old Liam used to do things like this all the time. Liam came into the room wearing a light grey collarless button-down and black slacks that fitted him like a glove. Both sisters rushed to him and started pestering him to tell them the plan. He hugged them and complimented them on how beautiful they looked. Ava was watching all this from a chair by the corner. She couldn't stop smiling at the excitement of the two sisters and the fondness in his eyes. How could he not be fond of them?, she thought, when they were both so lovely? In Ava's opinion, if anyone deserved this much love, it was her friend Liv. Liam spotted her in the corner and, with a flourish, offered her his hand to stand up.

"You're not asking where we're going?" he said.

"I enjoy being surprised."

"I hope you all like it," he replied, suddenly shy. She squeezed his hand in reassurance and the four of them left the house together.

"Are we picking up Scarlett?" Ava asked. Liam's steps faltered, and he froze for a second.

"She couldn't come," he said and resumed walking.

* * *

"What's this?" Nova asked in wonder. She was looking up, her eyes drinking in the whole place. From the outside, it looked like a regular warehouse, but inside it was like stepping into an enchanted forest. Trees with fairy lights and semi-translucent fabrics hanging covered the place. There were colorful banners and ribbons attached to the high ceiling, from where acrobats performed slow and sinuous dances. Barely covered jugglers moved about the place, their chests glistening in the low light. Nova was the most vocal about it, but she wasn't the only one with wide eyes and an astonished smile. Liv hugged Liam's right arm.

"I love it," she told him. He kissed the top of her head. A

waiter, dressed as what can only be described as a slutty fairy, offered them drinks from a tray. All drinks had impossible coolers - blue, green, purple - with glitter inside. They tasted sweet and bubbly and they kept coming.

There were different stages throughout the space, each one with a different performance: burlesque, acrobatics... In the center stage, the biggest one, a gorgeous woman, her dark skin shining under the stage lights, sang ethereal songs that were almost hypnotic. There were drinks, beautiful people, and endless wonders all around them. It was intoxicating.

A tall stranger took Nova to the dance floor and soon someone else took Ava. Liam turned to Liv. "Shall we?" he said, offering to dance, but Liv was looking over his shoulder, a cheeky smile on her face.

"Tonight, brother, we're in an alternative reality." And she pushed him into the arms of a stunning woman. Her black hair reached almost to her bottom—and the hem of her dress. By the way she looked at Liam and grabbed his hips, she also thought he was stunning.

After a few dances, he extricated himself from the dance floor and grabbed a drink from a passing tray. He searched for his sisters and found them both still dancing their hearts out. This had been a good idea, he thought. He tipped his head to finish his drink when something above him caught his eyes; an acrobat, but something was different about this one. He recognized her hair first, that long and wavy brown mane. She moved with grace, like the other acrobats, but she was more sensual. Her jumpsuit wasn't designed for this. The plunging neckline opened up and he could see the edge of her bra. The trousers, already short, let him see glimpses of more skin that he should be seeing. He finally understood what was different about her. She wasn't ethereal like the others, a dream from another reality. She was real, very real.

He thought he should look away—this was his little sister's friend after all—but for the life of him, he couldn't. Without taking his eyes from her, he took another drink and downed it in two gulps. He could almost, almost, imagine what it would feel like to… Nova took him out of his trance when she stumbled out of the dance floor.

"Oh, my God, that's Ava," she shouted. Liam looked down immediately and found three empty glasses in his hands. When had he drunk the third one? Those drinks were sweet, but definitely packed a punch, he decided. Otherwise, he couldn't explain what had just happened. He got rid of the glasses and spotted Ava walking towards them. She was back in her stilettos, having removed them to perform, and he couldn't stop staring at her legs. Nova intercepted her and grabbed both her arms. "That was incredible," she said. "How do you know to do that?"

"She did that at a college party," Liv piped in, having joined their group. "I swear she got invited to every party afterward, but she never did it again."

"It would get tired quickly. You can only surprise people with something like this once," Ava replied. Liam doubted anyone would ever tire of watching her perform. He forced himself to take his eyes from her, only to look back again when she spoke.

"Mmm, guys, have you noticed how the party is heating up?" Ava said. The three siblings looked around them and saw what Ava meant. The lights were dimmer, the acts a bit more daring and the guests more… free.

"Maybe it's time to leave," Liv said.

"Which client did you say gave you these tickets?" The three women looked at him, smiling knowingly. He cleared his throat to tell them he had no idea it was going to be like that when Ava interjected.

"She or he obviously didn't know your brother very well." Liv and Nova giggled.

"What does that mean?" he said, pulling himself up. Nova grabbed his arm.

"Let's go, bro. The midnight bells are ringing." He let go of her hand and frowned at them.

"Who said anything about leaving?" Slowly, he unbuttoned the first button of his shirt and lost himself in the throng of bodies on the dance floor. Nova whooped loudly and followed him.

"What's gotten over him?" Liv asked her friend. Ava was looking at him, jumping up and down, surrounded by women. She smiled and shrugged. The night was young, and so were they.

The next day Liv was ecstatic—also hungover—but mostly ecstatic. She couldn't stop commenting on the night before. Ava, impervious to hangovers, headaches, and general pains, was driving them both to their morning appointment. It was time for the final hair and makeup test. Liv opened the car window and let the air ease her headache.

"I don't remember when it was the last time I had so much fun," Liv said. "Maybe since college? But Nova and Liam weren't there. With them both… maybe… since Liam took over the business." For a moment, she had lost some of her energy, thinking about her parents, but she recovered. "I told you Old Liam was fun," she said.

"Who knew your brother could dance like that? You three together on that dance floor was something to behold. You're lucky I have high self-esteem because you and your family are unfairly good-looking. Your brother used to compensate with the temper of an eighty-year-old man, but yesterday he was just the perfect man. I hope it doesn't last or I won't be able to function."

* * *

LUCKILY FOR AVA'S SANITY, Old Liam lasted less than 24 hours. New Liam came back quickly when he found out about some changes done to the table arrangement.

"You cannot sit these people together. That's the business table and those are your friends. Change it all back," he demanded.

"But they're so boring," Liv said. "And they're your friends, not mine. It only makes sense to have them with your business contacts."

"You won't change them?" Liam asked, astonished. It wasn't that Liv never voiced her opinion, but never in direct opposition to him. Other people wouldn't even have considered that she was opposing him, but for mild-mannered Liv, that was almost a confrontation. He crossed his arms and huffed. He immediately assumed the source of her sister's attitude. "It just happens that they were sitting at Ava's table before. What a coincidence."

"It wasn't like that," Liv replied. "It's just a simple change, Liam."

"We'll see about that."

* * *

THE PROBLEM WAS that Liam wasn't sure where Ava was. He searched for her at the library, at the usual spot where she sat to read. He stormed into the room and glared at her reading nook, but she wasn't there. It was a bit of a letdown. Her next favorite place in the house was the kitchen, but he couldn't barge into it and startle Sandra. Instead, he opted to come in with slow steps, hands behind his back, and a formidable scowl on his face. Ava wasn't there either. Sandra thought he had a stomachache and offered him a chamomile tea. He tried the swimming pool with the same level of success - which was none. Finally, he tried her room. He definitely couldn't go into her room like a madman, and he had no other choice but to knock politely. It really diminished the whole 'I'm furious' attitude he was going for.

She was laying down in bed with her laptop on her legs. For the first time, Liam wondered what she did for a living. He had assumed she was a kind of hippie, moving from place to place with her old backpack and working odd jobs to sustain herself. However, her laptop was too expensive for that lifestyle. He would know, he had the same one, only an older version. They didn't sell those to individuals, so her company must have provided it. A remote worker then, but doing what? Ava asked her what he wanted, and he remembered he was mad at her. He put his arms behind his back and glowered at her. Her eyes lit up.

"Oh, my, you're angry," Ava said. "Do you need to unwind a bit?" She closed her laptop and put it beside her on the bed. She then put her hands in her lap and focused all her attention on him. He proceeded to tell her—in detail—how she was overstepping her boundaries and messing with Liv's wedding. He also added some colorful descriptions about what he thought of her attitude in life and how she had disrupted the peace in the house.

"That was pretty impressive. I'm not sure you even took a single breath. How long have you had that bottle up? I bet you feel much better now."

His face went completely red.

"Have you listened to anything I've said?"

"Of course I have. Not that I agree with most of it. It was Liv's choice to change the seating arrangement. She really dislikes that couple, you know? Don't ask me why as I don't know them. She had been wanting to do it for the longest time." Liam stood in the middle of her room, dumbfounded. He vaguely recalled Liv saying they were boring, but he hadn't understood what Liv had actually meant. Did she hate them? And he had forced her to invite them? Well, she could have said that before. Except that… had she tried? No, he would have remembered that. But this was Liv… He rubbed the side of his neck.

"She should have told me," he said. All heat had left his voice. He sounded more like a pouting child.

"I believe she just did," Ava replied.

"I mean before making a decision."

"Why? It's her wedding," she said.

"Because it's the polite thing to do," he replied, moving his arm in a slashing motion through the air.

"Why?"

"Because I'm her brother,"

"Why does that mean you need to be involved in her wedding decisions?"

"It's a family thing," he replied.

"Why, Liam?"

"Fine, have it your way. Both of you can plan the rest of the wedding without my help."

"Huh, it's funny. People always tell me I should think before speaking, that I sometimes let my anger carry me away. I never knew what they meant until now."

"I'm not angry," he pouted as he crossed his arms. Realizing how it looked, he uncrossed them and put his hands in his pockets.

"I never said you were," she replied.

"Do you always need to have the last word?"

"Not invariably, no. I'll let you have the last word now, if it means so much to you." Still lying on the bed, she crossed her legs and looked at him with an air of innocence. Against his will, he felt his mouth quirk up. He tried to smother it with a hand. He left the room grumbling something that sounded almost like "go to hell".

11 days with Ava

T hey were in their fifth shop, looking for the perfect paper for the seating arrangement. Liv always had a very artistic and crafty side, and she could tell the difference between each of the papers they had seen. And apparently, none of them was what she was looking for. Ava never complained of physical pains, but when Liv couldn't find the paper she wanted in the fifth shop either, Ava was reaffirming her belief that marriage wasn't for her—or at least weddings. She didn't think she could muster enough interest in paper.

After almost two weeks with Liv, she had also realized that her friend's life at that moment consisted exclusively of wedding preparations and Mason. They had talked briefly about Liv's last job, but Liv hadn't made a reference yet to what she was doing after the wedding. She wouldn't judge her friend if she chose to be a housewife, but she suspected that her friend had simply not thought about it. And that wasn't like Liv at all. In college, Liv always had a plan and schedule, just like her brother.

"Last shop, I promise," Liv told her friend as they got in the car.

"As many as you need."

"I like the second one in that shop, but they don't have it thicker and I don't want it to be see-through. If in the next one we find nothing better, I'll go back for this one."

"It's quite impressive to see you in the shops. You could be a wedding planner after this."

Liv gave a hollow laugh and took the car on the road.

"I'm sure there are people way more qualified than me."

"Who cares? You have the talent, a business degree, and contacts. You could be a success."

"I don't know about that."

Ava changed topics until they arrived at the new shop. She was actually quite surprised they were so many fancy stationery shops in this town, but maybe wealthy people needed more expensive papers. Liv seemed stuck with two different papers this time. One of them had the thickness she wanted, but the color was cream rather than off-white. She had each paper in one hand and she kept looking at each other.

"What do you think, Ava?" She passed both papers to her friend. Ava inspected them on both sides and one next to the other.

"I'd go for the heavier one. The color is not what you wanted, but the weight and texture are. I think it's the closest to your vision." Liv grabbed the paper in question and checked it further. Finally, she said she was happy with that option and passed it to the shop assistant. They discussed the amount, price, and delivery times until all was agreed.

As the store door closed behind them, Ava asked Liv, "What now?" Liv checked her list and declared they were free for the day.

"Shall we go for a walk?" Ava suggested. There was a park

nearby. "Do you remember when we were in college and we had all those plans and dreams?" Ava said.

"Well, you fulfilled your dream."

"I did, yeah. I'm sure you'll achieve yours soon." Liv crossed her arms, despite being a warm day.

"I'll be happy if I can pull off this wedding first."

"I'm sure it'll be fine and you'll be ready for your next project." They were passing by a fountain and the breeze was blowing some water droplets their way. It felt refreshing and they circle around the fountain to cool down.

"Can you lend me some of your confidence?" Liv asked.

"I'll lend you anything you want, my dear."

The problem, Liv thought, is that she didn't know what she wanted. Her phone rang, and she saw on the display that it was Mason. He had a discount coupon and wanted to invite her to lunch.

"Do you terribly mind?" she asked Ava.

"Of course not. Don't be silly. I'll see you at home tomorrow."

Liv happily pushed all thoughts of her future aside and joined Mason.

* * *

LIAM WAS SITTING at his desk in the library. A gigantic pile of mail lay unopened to his rights, with an even bigger amount of already opened envelopes sitting on his left. The letters were mostly bills. Who receives anything else in the mail anymore? There were some cards for Liv that she must have not seen, so he put those on the side to give them to her later. He was almost finished when he saw an invoice for something he didn't remember ordering. And it was a hefty one as well. He frowned and rechecked the items. He then noticed the letterhead. It wasn't for him. He was furious.

He stomped around the house until he found Nova by the pool. He showed her the invoice.

"Are you crazy?" he said. It wasn't really a question. Nova jumped from the lounge chair and took the letter from him.

"What are you doing going through my mail?"

"It was in my pile. But don't play dumb. What is that?"

"None of your business." Nova walked around him and entered the house.

"Where are you going? We're not finished."

"I'm going to recover the rest of my mail from your pile." She added quotation marks in the air in the last part of the sentence. Liam followed her upstairs to the library.

"How do you plan on paying for that? Not with your trust fund money, that's for sure. I told you that money won't be touched until you graduate from college." Nova swirled around and almost bumped into him.

"It's my money," she said, shouting.

"I won't let you throw it away," he said back, his voice matching hers.

Nova crossed her arms over her chest.

"You're like a broken record, but it doesn't matter. I'll make this company work, no matter how much you try to block it. I don't need the stupid trust fund money. I've found other ways."

"What other ways?" he asked. She scoffed.

"As if I'd tell you." Liam's face lost all color.

"What have you done?"

"I did nothing shady, you asshole. I just found an investor."

"Already?"

"Yes, already," she replied with a smug smile. "Someone that believes in me more than my own brother does." Liam's shoulders deflated.

"I believe in you, Nova, but why can't you wait until you

graduate? Live some more before facing the business world. I just want to protect you." Nova hesitated, but she squared her chin and straightened her back.

"Why should I when I've already found what I want to do?"

"You're so damn stubborn," he replied as he passed his hands through his hair, messing it up.

"I got it from you."

"You have to graduate!"

"I don't have to do a damn thing!"

They heard the front door and stopped their fight. Scarlett called hello from the entrance.

"Up here," Liam replied.

Scarlett joined them and kissed Liam. She smoothed his frown line.

"What are you both doing here?" Both siblings looked at each other with guilty looks. They didn't enjoy fighting with each other, but they always found themselves doing so.

"Liam found some mail of mine and he was going to give it to me," Nova said. Liam looked at her with narrowed eyes. "There better not be more invoices in that mail," he thought, "or they were going to have the same conversation again."

"Let's go," Liam told Scarlett. He put his hand on the small of her back and guided her towards the library. "Are you coming?" he asked Nova over his shoulder.

"I need the toilet." And she left.

* * *

SCARLETT AND LIAM entered the room together, only to find Ava reading in her usual spot. Liam was sure she had heard his fight with Nova. Again. It bothered him. He knew he was being harsh with Nova, but he just couldn't help getting angry every time she mentioned dropping out of college. Scarlett was oblivious to what had happened a few minutes before, so she greeted Ava with enthusiasm and Ava replied in kind. When had they become such good friends? Both women were talking about books. Scarlett was an avid reader and, judging by the time Ava spent in the library, she did, too. Scarlett had already read the book Ava had in her hands and they were comparing opinions on it so far. Liam sat down, thankful that they were distracted and Ava couldn't bring up how he had shouted at Nova. Except that he knew by now she wouldn't bring it up, not in front of someone else. She reserved her judgment for when he was alone. Both women continued chatting, oblivious to his brooding mood. Ava laughed at something Scarlett said.

He put his elbows on his knees and interlocked his hands. He could almost hear what Ava would say, that he was giving Nova unwanted advice. Well, so was her opinion. Not that she ever gave her opinion without being asked. He could give her that. Well, he wasn't planning on asking. He wasn't. What he wanted to say wasn't really a question, but it irked him she had heard that conversation without knowing the full story.

"What I said to Nova," he said. Both women turned to him. "I'm just trying to explain to her how difficult it is to start a company. She doesn't understand."

"What did you say to Nova?" Scarlett asked. Ava, however, said nothing. She kept looking at Liam, feigning innocence. Liam replied to Scarlett but kept looking at Ava, trying to gauge her reaction.

"I told her that being an entrepreneur isn't as exciting as films make it seem. It's a lot of hard work and sleepless nights. She should stay in college and enjoy her twenties." Scarlett's mouth opened in a silent 'oh'. She knew about the ongoing fight between her fiancé and her sister.

"So you're not happy with your life? Is that what you're

saying?" Ava asked. She cocked her head to the side, waiting for his answer.

"That's not what I said."

"I'm pretty sure it is," she said. Liam rubbed a hand on his face.

"If you only knew what a headache it is to start a company, you wouldn't encourage her."

"What are you talking about?" Nova said from the door. She had come in right after Ava's question. "Ava is the founder and sole owner of Ortech," Nova added. Both Liam and Scarlett looked at Ava with equal looks of astonishment. To Ava's credit, she didn't smile in satisfaction, even if she felt like doing so.

"Ortech? The electric car motor?" Liam asked.

"Not a whole motor, just a component," she replied.

"Yes, the part that makes it go for weeks with a single charge," Nova said. "Like the one in your car, Scarlett. It's called Ortech after her - Ortiz tech. Ava Ortiz."

"Didn't you study with Liv?" Liam asked.

"We did. We had some business classes together, but my major was in engineering."

"Why didn't you say something earlier?"

"I find people that brag about their accomplishments all the time absolutely insufferable," she replied. A ferocious glint showed in his eyes.

"Or perhaps you were happy to let us dig our own grave," he said.

"That would be extremely petty of me. And anyway, I find that in business there's always so much to learn that I'm happy to listen to other people's experiences." Liam gave a short laugh. Scarlett watched the two of them arguing. She was a very smart woman, and she knew their words went beyond their meaning, but she was struggling to understand what was really being said. She just had the vague feeling that she didn't like it, so she jumped into the conversation the only way she could see.

"That's very gracious of you. And you're right, of course. Nobody likes pretentious people," she said.

"Don't be a fool, love. There's nothing remotely gracious about what she did," Liam said. He leaned forward. "So Ortech, huh? How big is it? 50 billion?"

"Are we putting our companies on the table and measuring them?" Ava turned to Scarlett. "Don't listen to him," Ava said to her. "Not just in this conversation, but in general. I find that entitled men have very little to say that it's of any use."

"Entitled?" Liam said. His voice came out higher than his usual tone. Ava just smiled. "Entitled?" he repeated. Instead of replying, she left the room with Nova, never looking back.

* * *

Nova and Ava spent the rest of the afternoon together in the swimming pool. Both of them could talk for hours and the conversation felt comfortable. Films, books, business, climate change... they switched from one topic to another as if they had been friends for years. Nova wasn't sure if she was so comfortable because she had heard many stories about her from Liv, or because they had truly clicked, but it felt nice to have someone to talk to at home. Liv had been busy with the wedding and Mason for some time, and Liam, well, Liam still treated her as the seventeen years old she was when their parents passed away. Liv could have explained to Nova that this was one of Ava's talents. She could chat with a rock and make the rock tell her all its hidden secrets. Not that Ava wasn't enjoying her time with Nova—she was—but she didn't give that much thought to their easy interactions.

She liked Nova, and she was happy to spend that afternoon with her.

Liv was out with Mason and they weren't expecting her until the next day, but she surprised them all by getting back before dinner. She explained that Mason had an early start, and she wanted to let him sleep.

"Early start?" Nova snorted. "To do what?" Liv resented the question. Mason lived off his parents' allowance, but that didn't mean he didn't have projects. She didn't know what specific project had him waking up early, but neither did Nova.

"Has Sandra prepared any dinner or shall we do some takeaway?" Liv said, ignoring her sister's question. Sandra came out at that moment.

"I made dinner, and there's enough for you, too. Not that there should be, since you said you were eating out." Liv gave her a peck on the cheek and went to put the table. "Put five plates. Scarlett is staying too," Sandra told Liv before leaving for the day. Nova and Ava went to change out of their bikinis before dinner.

On the way back downstairs, Ava bumped into Liam. They continued their way together, taking the stairs in sync. Liam cleared his throat.

"Come on," he said, "you're dying to laugh. You made a fool of me today."

"I believe you did that on your own," she replied.

"Ouch," he said as he touch his chest as if hit by an arrow. "Still, you were happy to let me dig my grave. You should have told me the first time we spoke about it that you had your own company."

"You're absolutely right. I sincerely apologize for what I did. I promise I won't forget any of this in the future," she said. He was looking at her with narrowed eyes. "Why are you looking at me like that? Don't you believe me?"

"I just didn't expect you to apologize so easily," he replied.

"I'm right often enough that I can be gracious when I'm wrong." He laughed.

"I knew you had to have the final say. Anyway, let's forget about all this and join the family for dinner," he said. It was her turn to stare at him. "Why do you look at me like that? Is it you who don't believe me now?"

"I just didn't think you were so quick to forgive," she said.

"I've lost my temper often enough that I can understand when someone loses theirs."

"Perhaps you should try pilates," Ava said.

"Don't poke the tiger, Ava," he replied.

"Ha! A tiger, huh? That's one mighty comparison."

"You don't think I could be a tiger?"

"Well, you wear an excessive number of striped shirts." He looked down at his tailored shirt and suit with an affronted face.

"And I think you'd be a fox. The cunning and sneaky kind." When they both entered the dining room, the family was surprised to find them both laughing.

12 days with Ava

Nobody that knew Liam could have doubted that the party was going to be a success, but when a host has put so much effort, the polite thing to do is to stare in wonder as soon as you step into the house and post photos all over social media. Liam, Liv, and Nova couldn't really understand why someone would find their house so interesting as to take hundreds of photos of it, but they'd be lying if it didn't make them feel slightly proud. It wasn't just their house. There was something magical in the air that night. It seemed like the sky was darker and the lights in the house brighter, the people were better looking and the conversation more interesting than normal. Liv and Mason, arm in arm, greeted everyone coming in. Liam and Scarlett, arm in arm as well, were right behind them and they were, easily, the most stunning couple at the party. As people entered, they invited them to food and drinks.

"Come on, say it, everybody does," Nova said to Ava when she saw her looking at Liam.

"The two of them side by side quite take one's breath

away," she replied. "No wonder half the room is staring at them."

"The most annoying part is that she's as nice as she is beautiful," Nova added. Ava took a large gulp from her drink.

"How long have they been together?" she asked.

"About three years? They've been friends forever, but from what I understand, a few years ago she was having a bad time and he was there for her, and it just... sort of happened, I guess." Ava grinned and looked at Nova.

"What is it with your family and dating people that need them?" Nova blushed and looked away.

"What do you mean?"

"You too? Oh, boy, three for three," Ava laughed and looked towards Liam and Scarlett again. Her face sobered up. "Does that kind of relationship make you happy?" Nova followed the direction of Ava's eyes. Liam and Scarlett were greeting and smiling at an older lady, but as soon as she left, both their expressions changed and they turned around, not looking at each other. Then, another couple came to say hello and their mouths stretched into a smile again.

"It's hard to know what Liam thinks. Scarlett too. Over the past few years, they've changed. They've transformed into this perfect magazine couple that you see. Do they seem happy? If you ask me, Liam hasn't looked happy in quite some time, but I don't think it's Scarlett's fault. She told me once that she didn't know what she'd do without Liam. Theirs isn't just love, it's more complicated than that." Ava smiled, but for once, there was no happiness behind it.

"Well, I hope they are happy." She finished the rest of her drink in one go and took a deep breath. She put an arm around Nova's shoulders. "I believe this party is calling. Shall we?"

* * *

FOR THE SECOND portion of the night, they had hired a DJ and cleared the space in the large dining room. Liam grabbed a microphone and tapped on it twice, checking if it was working.

"Good evening," he said. People had been drinking already for a good portion of the night and perhaps they replied to his words with more enthusiasm than needed, but he wasn't going to complain. "This will be brief, as I'm not the star of this event. That role goes to Liv and Mason." He lifted his glass in their direction and everyone followed. Liv buried her face in Mason's chest, but you could see her shoulders shaking in laughter. In the distance, Liam saw Ava coming into the room and for a moment he lost his train of thought.

Ava stopped by the door and leaned on the doorframe, listening to him. She had followed the throng of people going into the dining room. She had heard a couple of women commenting on how hot Liam looked and, well, she had to see that for herself. Ava enjoyed looking at Liam almost as much as she enjoyed riling him. If that toast let her ogle him a bit and gave her ammunition to embarrass him afterward, it was a win-win. The two women she had overheard were whispering to each other and sniggering. Ava could tell they were making filthy jokes about him. This was perfect. She got closer to them, and she could hear one of them describing in very graphic detail what he could do to her. She could understand the other women's comments—he looked fantastic. Ava wasn't into suits, but the way Liam could carry one, she might become a fan of them after all. Liam continued with his speech, oblivious to the comments he generated.

"Those who know me can tell you that I'm not the most eloquent at this kind of declarations, but for you, Liv, I'd do this and much more. You deserve it all, sis. Every effort and every embarrassment and every raised glass. Mason," he said. He looked briefly at Ava, and his smile widened. "Please, make every effort to show my sister how much you love her every day, and how much you cherish her." There was a collective 'aww' from the guests. Liv was looking at her brother like he was handing her the moon. Mason was… rolling his sleeves. He approached Liam and took the microphone from him. Liv knew immediately what he was going to do and for a second she looked panicked, but she schooled her features quickly and smiled again.

"Liv, your brother is right. You deserve to hear every day how great you are. Because you're great, babes, the absolute best. I'll prove it to you… with a song." He whispered to the DJ and requested a base track to freestyle on top. He danced and improvised a rap song around Liv.

* * *

AVA LOOKED AROUND and caught Liam's eyes on the other side of the room. They looked at each other and suppressed a laugh. Slowly, both of them walked around the room until they were standing side by side.

"You did this on purpose," she told him as she pursed her lips, trying to hold it in.

"That would make me an exceedingly bad person." She snorted and tried to cover it with her hand and a cough. "It is not my fault that Mason is so predictable. Also, are you saying he's making a fool of himself?"

"I would never say that; it's such an unimaginative way of describing what he's doing." She rocked her head from side to side, thinking. "Training to withstand Guantanamo Bay torture?"

"Animal being tortured?" Liam offered. They both shook their heads. That wasn't it.

"The sound of delusion?"

"Sound, image, and smell of delusion," Liam sniggered. He took a sip of his drinks and leaned back on the wall. Mason singing and dancing were as insufferable as always, but this time, he couldn't help smiling.

"Gosh, can you imagine how his orgasm sound?" Ava blurted. Liquid went through Liam's nose and he almost sprayed the woman in front of them. Ava patted his back to prevent him from choking.

"That's an image I didn't need."

"I have it worse. I have a very vivid imagination." She faked a shiver.

Mason came to the end of his song, and everybody clapped. The DJ started playing again, and the room went back to dancing. Ava and Liam stayed standing side by side, neither of them moving. Liam wasn't sure if Ava wanted him to ask her to dance. Ava wasn't sure Liam knew how to dance. Finally, Liam moved away from the wall and extended his hand towards Ava, asking for a dance, but she wasn't looking at him. A guy, one of Mason's friends, had approached her and was asking her to dance, too. What was his name? Tom, he remembered now. Little piece of shit. She followed him onto the dance floor with a little wave to Liam. He put his hands in his pockets and stayed put, but after a few seconds, he felt silly standing there on his own and went searching for Scarlett.

* * *

LIAM WENT through every single room on the bottom floor, but he couldn't find Scarlett anywhere. She wouldn't have left without telling him. Perhaps she was upstairs? He checked the library. It would be the perfect place to rest for a bit. He would have enjoyed a rest himself. However, she was nowhere to be seen. There was no way he could have missed her. He'd recognize her anywhere. As a last resort, he checked his room, but she wasn't there either. He looked through his room window, trying to think where she could be when she saw her in the back garden. She was talking to someone he didn't recognize. He was too far away to see his face properly.

* * *

THE CHILL of the night cleared his head of some of the tiredness he wasn't aware he was feeling. He waved a hand to Scarlett and shouted her name, but she didn't hear him, too focused on the conversation. She was bracing herself with both arms. She must be feeling cold, Liam thought. In front of her was a man, but Liam couldn't see his face.

Scarlett finally looked his way and saw him. Liam smiled and inclined his head in salute. The other man turned around to see what had caught her attention. Liam faltered in his step when he recognized him. It was the man from the coffee shop, Ava's friend. What was his name? Phil. He had hoped to never see him again. There was something he really hated about that guy. He had promised Ava he'd be nice to him, but there was just something about him that irked Liam. Phil gave him a half-smile and put his hands in his pockets, adopting a relaxed posture, as if he knew exactly what Liam was thinking.

"Nice to see you again," Phil said as Liam reached them. "Cool house you have."

"Thank you, but it's not your first time here. Or did you forget when I found you hugging Ava in the library?" Liam put a hand on Scarlett's lower back, but then he removed it. He was never possessive with her. He didn't know what had caused it. Or rather, he didn't know what part of Phil was bringing it out.

"Scarlett and I were discussing how we knew each other," Phil said. Liam looked at Scarlett and raised his eyebrows. She hadn't told him that he knew Phil that first time at the coffee shop.

"We went to the same college," she said. She was smiling, but it didn't reach her eyes. He didn't know if she directed the fake smile at Phil or him.

"Yes," Phil said. "We were discussing some mutual acquaintances."

"Such a small world," Liam said. "And you both end up invited to the same party." Phil didn't reply to Liam's unspoken question and Liam had the feeling that he knew the answer. He was crashing at the party. Ava wouldn't have invited him without Liv's say-so, and since Liv had been there when he had met them, she would have known he hadn't liked him. Unless he was a friend of Mason. But he was older than him, and they hadn't been to the same school or college. Liam knew this because Mason had gone to the same ones as Liam.

"Maybe it was fate," Phil replied. "On that note, I believe another drink is in my future. Thanks for the lovely party, Liam. It was lovely talking to you, Scarlett. I hope to see you again soon."

When Phil left, Liam took Scarlett's hand.

"Was he bothering you?" he asked.

"No, I'm fine."

"Care to dance for a bit?" Scarlett didn't reply. Liam regarded her for a moment. She was looking into the garden, away from the party and him, with an expression he couldn't read. He thought by now he could always read her face. "You must be tired," he told her. "Do you want to rest a bit in my room?" That brought her out of her thoughts.

"No, it's fine. Let's go dancing."

As they walked into the house, Scarlett held onto his arm. Her high heels made it difficult to walk on the grass. Liam opened the door, but Scarlett stopped him.

"Maybe I do need to rest a bit. I don't think I'm ready to go back to so many people."

"Sure." He accompanied her to his room and offered her a blanket to cover herself with. She must have gotten chilly standing in the garden for so long.

When he returned to the party, Liam tried to find Phil again, but he must have already left. Yep, he had definitely crashed the party. Maybe Ava could shed some light on the guy because Liam certainly did not know what he was about.

* * *

AVA WAS ABOUT to join a group of friends when a hand on her waist stilled her.

"Your necklace is caught in your hair," Liam said, coming from behind her back. "Allow me." With gentle movements, he gathered her long wavy hair and pulled it over her left shoulder. A finger pried loose the small hairs at the nape of her neck that had gotten caught in the necklace. "Let me know if I'm hurting you," he said. Ava could feel his knuckles running through the back of her neck, unusually warm.

"That tickles," she giggled.

"Shhh, be still. I can't see what's wrong with the latch." His face got closer to see in the dim light of the room. His breath raised goosebumps on her neck. She tried to look over her shoulder, but a hand on the side of her face stilled her. "I told you to not move."

"I can't help it," she replied. "This feels too nice." He snorted.

"Do you always need to say everything that crosses your mind?"

"Otherwise, how will anyone know what I'm thinking?"

"Yeah? And what are you thinking now exactly?" he asked. His hot breath caressed the back of her neck and she wasn't sure it was an accident.

"That Tom's offer is becoming more appealing by the second." Ava heard a loud snap and a grunt.

"Have mercy on that poor boy," Liam said as he took her hair and placed it against her back again. Ava smiled as she felt his hand sliding all the way down her back before Liam stepped to her side.

"Boy? He's at least as old as you, positively ancient," she replied. She had an empty glass in her hand. He quickly replaced it with a new one and left the old one on a passing tray. He moved to her side, and they stood watching the party.

"I'll have you know I'm in my best years," Liam said. "I'm emotionally mature and physically stronger than ever." He tried to keep a straight face during their banter and failed miserably.

"Oh, so maybe that poor boy, as you called him, is worth an opportunity."

"Please, you'll chew him up. You'll be bored with him after five minutes," he said.

"And then what type of man should I go for?" She looked at him while she asked, and he returned her stare. For a few breaths, none of them said a word. He averted his eyes first.

"Maybe I was wrong," he said. "I'll put in a good word for you." She laughed and pushed him lightly to the side.

"Don't you dare. I've been trying to get rid of him for the past hour. He doesn't understand subtle hints," Ava said, and he chuckled.

"Oh, so you know how to be subtle?" he said. "He must be thicker than a brick."

"Don't be mean, he's oblivious," she replied.

"A man should know how to back off when his advances are unwanted." She raised her glass in a salute to him.

"To you, for taking rejections as all men should." He clinked his glass with her and leaned closer. He spoke right next to her ear.

"Oh, but I've never been rejected before," he whispered. She looked at his face up close: the full lips, the wrinkles around his eyes when he smiled, the lock of dark hair falling over his right eye. She got close to his left ear and whispered in turn.

"And now we know why you're such an ass." He laughed so hard some guests turned to look at them. "So," Ava said, "did you come to mock my taste in men?" Liam lost his smile, remembering his encounter with Scarlett and Ava's friend. He had come to ask her about him, but now talking about that guy was the last thing he wanted to do. He looked around until he saw a friend William, who waved at him.

"Excuse me," he murmured, "I think someone's calling me."

She watched him go and thought that apart from being an ass, he also had a nice one.

* * *

LIV AND AVA were making their way to the garden. Liv was sipping on a glass of water. They sat on the gazebo to relax a bit. Even with the garden door closed, they could still hear the music going on. The silhouette of Mason was visible through the glass, dancing in the middle of a circle of his friends.

"I'm so tired," Liv groaned. She rolled her neck from side

to side. Ava was still standing. She faced Liv and put her hands on her hips.

"I've suspected something since I met Mason," Ava said. She was very serious. She paused before continuing and took a deep breath. Liv opened her eyes wide. "Mason… Was he in a dance crew?" Ava asked. Liv threw her head back in laughter.

"No, but your guess is pretty close. When his album failed, he became a DJ. I guess he still is? Only for fun, though. He's not trying to be a professional. At least not anymore. He says it's a cruel world." Ava thought it must have been particularly cruel to someone without talent, but she kept those uncharitable thoughts to herself. "We met that way. Do you remember I told you? I bumped into him and he thought I was a groupie. He took out his sharpie and signed my chest. I didn't have the heart to tell him I didn't know who he was. He looked like he needed a fan at that moment. And here we are now."

"It's a long way to go just to avoid disappointing someone," Ava joked.

"I guess it is." There was something sad seeping through Liv's words that didn't escape Ava's notice. She stood up and dusted the back of her dress. She leaned on the veranda and put her elbows on it.

"The good thing is that you found each other. And he found someone that enjoys his musical numbers."

"You're mocking me," Liv said.

"No, I'm mocking him. But if you love him, none of it matters, does it?" A shadow crossed Liv's face, only to disappear in a second. She stood up as well and joined her friend.

"What about you, Ava? Have you found love?"

"I love my friends and my job. I love you, Liv."

"Don't ignore my question."

"You mean the love that you and Mason share?" Liv

stared at her friend and hesitated, but she didn't rise to Ava's veiled taunt. "Show me one love that it's unconditional," Ava said. "Show me a love that lifts you up and makes you feel invincible. Show me love unparalleled. Then, perhaps, I might consider it. But there isn't such a love, Liv. I haven't seen it." But as soon as she said it, an image flashed through Ava's mind. She shook her head to get rid of the vision. Liv gave her a sad smile.

"Ava, the love you describe as impossible is the love that you give everyone you know." She stepped down from the gazebo. "Shall we rejoin the party?"

"I'll stay here a bit longer," Ava replied. "I still feel too hot. Look hot as well," she winked. Liv obliged her with a chuckle and left her friend alone.

* * *

NEARLY TWO HUNDRED people had shown up at the party and Liam felt like he had spoken to each one of them for hours. He needed to have a drink and sit quietly for a few minutes. He made his way quietly to the garden, trying to avoid being stopped for another chat until he saw Ava. She was leaning against the gazebo, looking into the house. She saw him approaching and immediately perked up. He stopped in front of her.

"I assumed you'd be still dancing until your pretty slippers wore off," he said.

"And I assumed you'd be looking at your calendar, checking what should be happening in the next ten minutes."

"Oh, please, I pay people to do that for me."

"I know that you still like to check your calendar for fun."

"That's not my definition of fun."

"Then what is?"

"You have me all figured out, don't you?"

She moved her head to the side and observed him.

"Let's make a bet. If you don't have the calendar of your phone color coded, I'll go back in and do a musical number to the song of your choice."

"And if you win?"

"You take Liv and Nova on a night out before the wedding," she said. "A wild night out," she clarified at his questioning face. "There has to be such a debauchery and abandon that you have to stay the next morning in bed nursing the hangover of all hangovers."

"Nothing for you?" he asked.

She extended her hand and made a forward motion, indicating he should give her his phone. He opened his jacket and, slowly, made a show of getting it from the inside pocket. He handed her the device, but didn't let go when she grabbed it.

"You still have time to change your side of the bet," he said. She just smiled and, with a small tug, took his phone. She slid the screen up and pointed it at him to unlock the phone with face recognition. With a couple of taps, she opened his calendar. He was looking at her, hands in his pockets, with a small smile. She looked up and gave the phone back.

"So, what will I be performing tonight?" she asked. He made a show of thinking about it. He rubbed his chin, his hands, walked around Ava.

"Mmm, let me think. There are so many good options: Anaconda from Nicki Minaj." He looked at her face, trying to see what song made her react. "My Hump from Black Eyed Peas." Ava, however, knew what he was trying to do, so she just remained calm. "My Neck, My Back." He stopped with this one. He almost asked her to sing that one, but he wasn't sure how some of the party guests would react. Then he had an idea. "Tell me, Ava, how well can you sing?" She just snorted. His answering smile was so feral it could scare a child.

* * *

AVA TOOK the microphone from the DJ booth and tapped on it a few times. Most guests went quiet and turned to her.

"As you all know, tonight we've gathered on the occasion of my dear friend Liv's upcoming nuptials." The guests all cheered. "To celebrate it, I want to sing in honor of the lucky couple what it is, probably, one of the best well-known love songs of our time. I hope you all enjoy it. Liv, my dear, this one is for you."

And then she sang My heart will go on, by Celine Dion, in what was probably one of the worst renditions to date. Ava knew she was a terrible singer, but she also had very little sense of ridicule, so she belted those notes and twirled around the room with so much confidence that she had the entire room clutching their bellies in laughter. When she finished with a bow, the room clapped and whooped, demanding another one. And if Liam's voice was louder than the rest, nobody seemed to notice.

* * *

ABOUT HALF AN HOUR LATER, Scarlett went to say goodbye to Liam. She wasn't feeling well. Liam rubbed her arm, making sure she was OK to drive on her own. "I can take you, if you want," he said. She kissed him and assured him she was fine. "I think I just ate too much." He walked her to her car, holding the driver's door open. Liam debated if he should still go with her. He didn't want to leave her alone if she was feeling poorly, but there were still a couple of hours left at least at the party, and he didn't want to seem rude.

"I prefer to go on my own," Scarlett said, reading his dilemma. "I'll get home and go straight to bed." He bit his lip, still unsure.

"Will you call me if you need me?"

"I promise," she said as she kissed him goodbye.

He was still thinking about Scarlett as he returned to the party when he bumped into someone.

"Hey Lewis, are you leaving already?" Lewis was a childhood friend of Nova. He looked like a surfer, with sun-bleached blond locks and a permanent tan, even though he probably hadn't touched a board in his life. But it wasn't a look he cultivated. He had looked like that his whole life. Liam liked him. He had been a good friend of his sister, pulling her out of more than one scrap. And Liam knew how easily her little sister got into those.

"Yeah, I'm going to head out, but it has been an amazing party. Not that I doubted it would be." They shook-bumped fists in that way only young men seem to like. He was the only one that still did that to Liam. The rest of the world shook his hand.

"Thanks," Liam said. "Come over one day, OK?"

At that moment, Ava came out the door, adjusting her purse on her shoulder, and stood next to Lewis.

"I'm ready," she said.

"Ready for what?" Liam asked.

"Lewis is going to show me the town at night," she replied as she grabbed his arm. Lewis laughed softly and looked at her as if he couldn't quite believe his luck.

"Right now?" Liam asked. He could have kicked himself, but he couldn't take it back now.

"Is that OK?" Lewis asked, his eyes moving between Ava and Liam.

"It's Liv's party," Liam replied to Ava.

Instead of replying, Ava let Liam's words hang in the air.

Lewis was about to head back inside, but Ava had his arm tugged firmly in place and he couldn't move. She looked completely relaxed, but not even a bulldozer could move her from that spot.

"Forget I said anything," Liam said, cracking under the silence. He walked around them and disappear inside the house.

"What was that?" Lewis asked Ava.

"A man confused. Let's go."

<h1 align="center">13 days with Ava</h1>

For the past couple of days, Ava had been observing Nova. She was unusually quiet, and sometimes she'd get lost in thought in the middle of a conversation. She had also started to run far away from them anytime she had to answer a call. Ava wasn't close enough to Nova to be in her confidence. She thought about talking to Liv about it, but she could be mistaken and worry her friend for no reason. That day Liv had slept at Mason's and Liam had left early for work, so Ava and Nova had breakfast alone. Nova was inexplicably interested in her coffee. She kept staring into her cup and biting her right-hand nails. Ava asked her if she had plans and Nova jumped in surprise.

"Plans?" Nova asked.

"For today," Ava said. Nova relaxed when she understood Ava's question. She shrugged her shoulder and said she wasn't doing anything special.

Ava couldn't let her continue in that state. She was going to ask what was going on; it didn't matter that they'd only known each other for two weeks. She decided the direct approach was the best—not that she ever chose any other method. Ava wasn't very good at subtlety. Nova had finished her breakfast. She stood up and left the room as she checked her emails on her phone. Ava run after her, jumped up the stairs, and blocked Nova's way.

"Something's definitely wrong with you," she said. "And it's been happening for a few days."

"What? No, I'm fine," Nova replied. "I just need to take some iron."

"You don't look tired, you look anxious."

Nova visibly paled, but she shook her head and insisted it was nothing. She tried to move around Ava, but she touched her elbow. "I won't tell a soul," she promised, "but I can't see you moping around anymore. Give me the chance to help, even if it's by listening." Nova opened her lips and just stayed there with her mouth open. She dropped her shoulder and sat down on the stairs, and buried her face in her hands. Ava sat down next to her. An investor had promised her some funding, Nova explained, and on the back of that promise, she had made some heavy spending.

"It was the money I needed to take the next step, but the investor pulled out."

"Was there anything signed?" Nova turned towards Ava and opened up her arms in front of her.

"He promised. I thought that was as good as signed. He's a reliable investor, I swear."

"I'm sure he is, but there might be several reasons why he decided not to invest in the end." Nova buried her face in her hands again and groaned.

"I need to find some funding and quickly. I thought about selling some of my things like my car and jewelry, but Liam would find out and he'll tell me I'm not ready to build my own company." Ava gently stroked her back.

"He might bark a bit, but he has no bite. He'd never let you shoulder all this on your own." Nova shook her head.

"I have to do this on my own or I'll prove him right. I don't want to fail before I even started." Ava gave a firm nod of her head.

"Good, that's the spirit. Let's do this. I know quite a few investors from dealings with my company. Send me your business plan and all your figures. I'll ask them to have a look and see if someone it's interested." Nova raised her head and looked at her. Her lips tremble, unable to decide if she had reasons to smile or not.

"Would you do that?" she asked, her face hopeful. "I don't want any favors, though."

"Darling, these people don't do favors. They're in it for the money. Either they believe you can make them money or don't. The only thing I'm doing for you is getting a reply out of them quicker, but I can't promise there will be good news. Now run upstairs and send me everything. When do you need to make the first payment?" Nova bit her lip.

"I really need to start paying this week."

"Hold off selling your pearls two more days and we'll see. Come on, we're on a deadline."

Nova jumped up the stairs two at a time. From the top, she shouted thank you to Ava and rushed to her room.

* * *

NOVA WAS BITING her nails to the quick, pacing around the room while Ava read.

"So? Do you think investors will be interested?" Ava lifted her eyes from the tablet where she was reading Nova's business plan and projections.

"Be still and take a sit. Never show them how much you need the money. You're selling them an opportunity, not asking them for a loan." Nova sat down at the edge of the chair, her back straight and her left leg jumping up and down. Ava smiled. "Nova, it's just me, and this is just practice. Seriously, relax." The younger woman smoothed down her shirt unconsciously and leaned back in the chair. "Now, this is good, Nova, but I'm going to make you a series of questions that will most likely come up with the investors. I assume you already answered them with the previous one, but it never hurts to be more prepared. Are you OK with that?"

"Yes, please. Be brutal if you need to be."

Ava spent the next hour dissecting Nova's business with her. Nova wanted to create a marketplace for local cooperatives and farms, providing them with cheap and easy access to technology to sell their products to a larger audience. It wasn't just an online marketplace; she had included options for extra revenue streams like tourist visits to the farms or venue hire. Her margins had to be small to make it worthwhile to the farmers and local artisans, so she had to achieve a large number of transactions on the platform before becoming profitable. That was her biggest risk. The business would need a couple of years of losses before starting bringing in enough profit.

"Retail is not my specialty," Ava said while reading Nova's plans, "but I've always wanted to learn more about it. I'm enjoying this."

"But do you think it has potential?"

"You're really passionate about this, aren't you?" To Ava's surprise, Nova blushed in response. Ava suspected there was a story behind this business idea, but she didn't pry. "I'll let you know what the investors say." Nova jumped from her chair and enveloped Ava in a tight hug.

"I don't know how to repay you."

"You don't need to, dear. Now go and find something to distract you or you'll be fretting all day."

* * *

AVA SPENT the rest of the morning ensconced in the library with her laptop, making calls. Nova, trying to distract herself, went to the gym and spent two hours on the treadmill blowing off some stress. When she went back at midday, she knocked on the library door to ask Ava if she could help her. She felt guilty about having Ava work on this all morning. Ava simply smiled and told her an investor was interested.

"Check your bank account tomorrow."

"So quickly?" Nova wasn't sure, but she had the impression that reaching for investors was a lengthier process. She had achieved one in six months, and that had turned out to be a fluke. Now she got one in a day?

"I guess someone really believes in that project," Ava replied.

14 days with Ava

W hen Nova woke up the next morning, she was still in a haze. Also tired, she was very tired. Later the day before, Ava had sent her an email with seven documents attached. She had spent hours reading them in detail, well into the night, to make sure she understood the suggested agreement with the investor. She couldn't believe Ava had secured investment so quickly. It had taken her months to secure that failed investment. It made her feel a bit of a failure, but she shoved that feeling to the bottom. If she was going to make this company a success, she couldn't second guess herself.

She was now on her way to the bank to speak with her financial advisor to make sure everything was correct. Despite the lack of sleep, her feet barely touched the ground. She wasn't losing her company.

She hadn't had time to make an appointment, but the advisor managed to squeeze her in that morning. She and Nova knew each other from before and had a close relationship. It also helped that she was part of the Stewart family, although Nova was, in general, oblivious to the special treatment her surname gave her. The financial advisor read through all the documents and smiled at Nova.

"This is fantastic, Ms. Stewart. Congratulations on securing this investment."

"So, do you think I should sign them?" she asked. She would not make the same mistake as the first time. From now on, she was going to look through every agreement with a magnifying glass. The advisor offered her a pen in response. Nova took it with a smile and started signing the contract.

"If you don't mind me asking, Ms. Stewart, is there a chance I can be at the next meeting? I've always been an admirer of her."

"Of the investor? I don't know them directly. A friend got me in touch."

"Oh, I see. That's a shame. I've really wanted to meet her. What she did with those cars and the way she build such a successful company so young."

Nova stopped in the middle of signing the third copy of the contract. She wasn't sure she heard correctly.

"Did you say cars?"

"Yes. Do you know those electric cars that can run for days on a single charge? I'm jealous you're going to work with her."

Nova grabbed a glass of water from the table and took a big gulp. All the joy of finding an investor had abandoned her. Could she sign that contract now?

* * *

NOVA HADN'T VISITED her brother's office in a while. For a couple of years, when she was about to enter college, she dreamed of one day directing the company side by side with Liam. Perhaps even open an office overseas and help him expand even further their parents' legacy. That's how their parents had built the company, the two of them side by side, and Nova liked the idea of replicating their organizational model. However, when she finally convinced her brother to give her an internship, she realized she wanted something else. Their parents might have started the company, but her brother had made it entirely his own. He had taken the small factory the family had and built it into a multi-billion dollar company. Nova wanted to do the same. She wanted to create something of her own, not just piggyback on what Liam had achieved. She wanted to be like him, commanding, but fair, with vision, but also realistic. And if she wanted to be honest with herself, she also wanted his approval. Nova wanted Liam to look at what she had achieved and know that they were equals, that he didn't need to worry about his little sister anymore. But that dream was about to burst. With a knot in her stomach, she stepped into the building and requested at reception to see her brother. Rebecca, the woman that had been manning reception since the day her parents opened the building, greeted her with a smile and called Liam directly. Liam asked for her to come up.

Before opening the door, Nova took a deep breath and gave herself a small pep talk. She knocked lightly and waited. She expected to hear a muffled "enter", but instead, Liam opened the door with the biggest smile and gave her a hug. Nova was so confused by this reception that she didn't even return his hug immediately. This was an Old Liam hug, tight and warm, as if seeing you made him the happiest man alive. For a second, Nova thought she was going to cry. What Nova didn't know is that Liam's mind had been wandering in directions he was trying really hard to avoid and she had been a most welcomed distraction. He hadn't been able to do any productive work for the past twenty minutes and he practically jumped when Rebecca had told him that Nova was downstairs.

"Let's go down to the canteen," he said, stepping away from the hug. "Margaret has been asking me forever when you were coming to visit." He moved towards the door, but Nova was frozen on the spot.

"Liam, I'm in trouble," she said. He went serious and studied his sister's face.

"Alright, let's go inside my office." He shut the door behind them. Nova took a seat by the desk, put her elbows on the desk, and held her face in her hands. Liam stood by her side and gently put a hand on her shoulder.

"OK, tell me," he said softly.

Nova told him the whole story until the part where Ava became her chief investor. She paused and braced herself for his anger, but he just listened to her, his face neutral. When she finished telling him about the failed investment, he walked over to the window and looked out, his hands in his pockets.

"I never told you how it was when I took over the company, did I?"

"I know all about how you changed it and grew it, yes." He waved his hand.

"That's the PR story. Mum and dad, right before they passed away, were about to retire," he said.

"What? But they were still young. And this company was their thing, their baby." Liam shrugged his shoulders.

"I don't know their reasons. I only found out when I took over. They had sold already several parts of the company. The parts left were going through redundancies and restructures to make them more profitable and sell them at a good price. But I didn't want to sell." He took a deep breath. "Sometimes I wonder if I should have let it go and sell the rest as they wanted, but then, what would be of us? You know how I was back then. I didn't care about anything, just having a good time. I panicked that I could do nothing by myself, so I decided to keep what was left." Nova walked over to her brother and grabbed his hand.

"I didn't know," she said.

"Nobody knew. I haven't even told Scarlett. You know that I have my pride. Maybe too much, as Ava would say." Liam stopped at her name's mention. He had told someone, at least parts of it. He cleared his throat as if to dispel the thought. "I mangled it all when I started. I lost all my fund money. For a while, I had this immense debt. I thought I had cost us all our savings, and the house… I never touched your fund or Liv's," he clarified, "but the rest of it, I almost lost it all. It finally took off, but it was a near thing." He looked at his sister. "You've had a small taste of how badly things can go in a business, Nova. Do you still want to go ahead? I'll release your fund money, but I just need to make sure you know what you're doing. It won't be easy, sis. Are you ready for the worst-case scenario?"

Nova hesitated. "I… I didn't tell you everything," she said. "I don't need the funds. Ava found out I was in trouble and— I didn't ask her," she added quickly at his furrowed brow. "She—you know how she is. She had my business plan and, well, she told me she was going to send it to some investors she knows, but instead she invested in it herself. When I found out it was her I thought about rejecting it, but I was desperate and I signed. But after I left the bank, I thought about it again and I—I don't know what to do. Was it bad of me to take her money?"

Liam looked puzzled. He made Nova repeat everything. This time around, Nova felt calmer. Liam hadn't eaten her alive or, God forbid, shouted at her. She told the entire story —skipping no part—all over again. Liam sighed at the end and rubbed the bridge of his nose.

"I'm a bit hurt you didn't come to me sooner," he confessed. Nova buried her face in her hands.

"I know. Ava said I should talk to you from the beginning, but I just couldn't face your disappointment." He bent forward and took her hands in his.

"You can never disappoint me, sis. I know I'm sometimes a little forceful. Well, more than a bit," he added at her sister's expression. "I only want to save you the headaches I had to go through."

"I know."

"Ugh, now I need to go talk to Ava," he said as he messed his hair. Nova laughed. "Seriously, you and your sister need to stop having Ava sort out your messes. We owe her so many favors, I'll need to hand over this company to pay her back."

"We don't ask her to do it," she nearly shouted. "But she has a way of making everyone feel at ease with her. She feels like part of the family."

"At ease? At ease? We haven't had a moment of peace since she arrived."

"And yet I feel more at peace than I did before." Liam caressed his sister's cheek. "You too have changed recently, you know?" she told him. "You are more relaxed. More like the Old Liam."

"What an ogre must I have been to you two." Cutting off Nova's protest, he put his arm around her and finally led her to the canteen for a long break together.

* * *

"Where is Sandra?" Liam asked when he entered the kitchen and found Ava peeling some potatoes and their cook missing.

"I asked her to lend me the kitchen this one time. I

promised Liv I'd make her my famous chips once before I leave. We used to eat them all the time in the dorms." Liam's heart skipped a bit at the mention of her leaving, but he dutifully ignored it. Picking up a knife from the drawer, he started to help her.

"Is potato peeling one of your talents? You have so many I'm losing count," Ava said.

"Hilarious, but I'm not particularly good at it, as you can tell. I'm afraid I'll cut off my thumb." He was indeed doing a terrible job, peeling half the potato off along with the skin. "You know what I came to say, but I don't know if you'll allow me," he said.

"You're right, and I don't."

They were both so quiet they could hear the soft scratching of their knives. They were completely alone in the house.

"I can give you my car. You mentioned once it was a good way of repaying debts," Liam said.

"I'm sort of your family's boss now and I don't approve of your careless disposal of your assets." He chuckled.

"If you're going to consider yourself my boss, I'd rather Nova loses her company," she laughed, and he smiled in return. He then realized that every time she laughed or smiled, he couldn't help reciprocating. "I don't like feeling indebted to someone, you know?"

"Who does?" she replied.

"Then, please, let me know how I can repay you."

"OK, I'll tell you. You'll listen to Nova and support her in her startup."

He was quiet for the longest time. He left the knife and potato he was peeling on the counter and leaned on it.

"Do you really think she can make it?" he asked.

"Do you?"

He picked up again the potato and finished peeling it.

"I believe she can make it, but I don't know if I want her to suffer so much pressure. As you know, when I took over my parents' company, I really struggled. Some nights, I barely slept. So many people depended on me to keep it going, so many families that depended on the salaries my company paid."

"Back then, how many times did you wish your parents were there to support you?" He considered her question.

"I spoke to her earlier. She explained everything that had happened. I—I realized I was in the wrong. I thought she needed protection instead of support. But now I have changed my mind, and she now has access to her funds to do as she pleases. If you want, we can—she can return your investment."

"Absolutely not. I think she has a solid business idea and the drive to make it happen. I want stocks in that company. This wasn't charity. I don't play with my money. " He nodded with his head while he grabbed another potato to peel.

"If you won't let me give you anything for your help, let me at least say this. I haven't been the best brother for Liv and Nova and I fully acknowledge that. What you've done for Nova—and how—let's say that I believe that our relationship will be forever changed, for the better I hope, by your actions and words. Know the impact you've had on us."

"As usual, you're putting too much responsibility on your shoulders. Every family has some communication problems, but not all have the love you share. I can see, we all can, the fierce love you have for them. You're tyrannical sometimes—"

"And pigheaded," he added.

"That too," she laughed. "But it comes from a place of love, and they can feel that. You're good to them, but maybe sometimes you show it the wrong way."

He bit his bottom lip, pondering if he should ask what he had been wanting to ask for some time.

"You don't always have the best to say about families," he finally said, unsure if it was insensitive to ask directly. She, of course, understood what he really wanted to say.

"My parents divorced when I was fifteen," she said. He nodded in understanding. He knew it must have been a tough time. "They fought over everything, including who got to keep me."

"Did you have to choose?" he asked softly.

"No, no, you don't understand. Neither of them wanted to keep me. They wanted the other to take care of me." His head wiped towards her.

"What?"

"They left me with a flat for myself and a ridiculously high monthly allowance, and they both left town. I think they went traveling and partying—each on their own, of course. They had me young, so they needed to get something out of their systems, I guess."

"They left you alone?"

"I wasn't an easy child. Even back then, I said everything that crossed my mind and I think I told them some harsh truths about themselves that made them uncomfortable. When I was sixteen, I decided I was done being a burden, so I legally emancipated. We have a much easier relationship now. They're cool people."

"Are you seriously making excuses for them?"

"Not every family loves each other unconditionally, and I think I'm like my parents. Family wasn't for us. I'm saving myself some heartache and staying away from marriage. I'll live my best life and be the crazy aunt to Liv's children. When we're all in our eighties, I'll come to visit. I'll dress as if I were still twenty, and make outrageous propositions to men twenty years younger than me." He wasn't sure what to say. She told the story with complete detachment, but he had a hard time believing she was as unaffected as she sounded.

"You said you're not made to have a family, and yet you treat Liv as a sister. Even Nova, even though you just met."

"But that's because they are great people. I hate to see them suffer. If I see someone having a hard time, I just help them."

"And who helps you?"

"And who helps you?" she said back. "What you three have, that's special," she continued. He stopped peeling to look at her profile. She was staring into the distance. "Maybe if I had that, I could be in a family. A sister shouting at me for borrowing her clothes. Or someone calling me asking when I'm coming back home. Someone that talks to me about important stuff, not five-minute conversations to be polite." She looked at him and smiled, although it lack her usual enthusiasm. "You're one lucky person." He wanted to say so many things to her: how what she described is what a healthy family is, how it was within her reach and how she absolutely wasn't to blame for her parents' selfishness, but if the last few incidents with Nova and Liv have taught him is that sometimes people just want to be listened to. He didn't need to sort out their lives for them, just make them see that someone understood them.

"I am lucky," he replied simply, staring back at her. She finished peeling her potato and dropped it in a bowl full of water—and dozens of peeled potatoes. He frowned. "How many more potatoes do we need to peel?"

"Two more bags," she replied.

"Just how many people are coming over for dinner?"

"Some."

"I actually don't want to know," he replied while shaking his head. "Don't tell me your toy boy is coming. Actually, I take that back. It'll be kind of fun to see him chasing you around." She threw a potato peel at him.

"Lewis? That's over, I'm afraid. I'm not into puppy love. I prefer doggy style." She winked. He laughed and threw the potato peel back at her.

"Oh, yeah? And what do you look for in a man, then? Apart from deeply unimaginative positions."

"Who says I'm looking for a man?" she replied.

"Touché. Oh, Goddess of independence and female empowerment, if you ever decide to settle with a man, what would it take? No, wait, don't tell me, I can guess. He needs to be tall and have a six-pack, a tight ass, and a full head of hair. Oh, and the smile of a movie star. He needs to love cars, of course, but nothing too flashy. You prefer cars built for efficiency." She laughed.

"You believe me so shallow? Muscles disappear with age, but I hope love doesn't. I want someone smart, true, only because I can't spend all my life having dull conversations. I want someone healthy, someone that will stay with me for years because I'm planning to reach at least ninety-eight and I don't want to say goodbye before then. But what I really want is someone… reliable. I want someone I can count on and that would move the earth for his family because I'd move it for him. Someone that doesn't make me feel alone." Silence followed her answer.

"That was surprisingly deep," he said after a few beats. "I was expecting your usual levity."

"Well, I forgot to say I also want him to have a massive big d—" He put some raw potato in her mouth before she could finish her sentence. "Let's just say that you want someone perfect for someone perfect," he said, smiling. Suddenly, he realized what he had said and his smile disappeared. She wasn't smiling either. They stared at each other. He stretched his hand and pulled some stray hairs behind her ear.

"Liam…" she said.

"I've just gone and embarrassed myself." He looked at her for a few seconds until he visibly came to a decision. "But I meant it," he said. "I really do."

Liam approached Ava and slowly, giving her time to pull away, he leaned in from the side. He buried his face in the side of her neck and inhaled her deeply. He touched her hair. Liam had wanted to do that for the longest time. It always looked so soft and shiny. Ava closed her eyes. A distant clock in another room of the house faintly chimed the hour. A fly was buzzing against the terrace door. Liam's hand came around Ava and pulled her in through her waist. His lips touched her earlobe, and she visibly shuddered. He waited there, willing her to make the next move. He waited for her to respond. She touched his hand at her waist and squeezed.

"I know you're incapable of hurting another person," she whispered. Her words were like a punch to his stomach. He took a deep breath and stepped away from her.

"Yeah, I don't want to hurt anyone," he replied. She nodded once in understanding, a firm shake of her head. He cleared his throat and passed his hand through his hair, trying to compose himself.

"I should have come to visit the first time Liv invited me during college. I would have loved to meet the Liam that was free of responsibilities."

"I'm afraid you would have been sorely disappointed. I had to grow up fast when my parents died because I had done very little maturing in the twenty-five years before." She stretched her hand, avoiding getting any closer, and touched his cheek.

"Then I wish I could take some of your current responsibilities away now," she said. He breathed deeply, feeling the warmth of her skin against his face.

"And I wish you were one of them." She let go of him and resumed peeling potatoes.

"I have been no one's responsibility since I was sixteen," she said. "And I have been responsible for my own orgasms even before. What can I say? I'm self-sufficient like that." For once, her flippant comments failed to make him laugh. Instead, a hungry look had appeared in his eyes.

"Fuck, maybe you should stop going after little boys that don't know what they're doing."

"Maybe I like teaching them a few tricks," she replied, a challenge in her voice. He was about to reply, but thought better of it. Instead, he left the kitchen knife on the table and asked Ava to continue on her own. She watched him jog—actually jog—upstairs to his room with a sad smile.

* * *

LIAM WRAPPED a towel around his waist and dried his hair. He checked his watch. He had spent too much time in that shower. The steam of the shower still lingered in the bathroom air. He wiped the mirror and stopped. What an idiot he had been. What had possessed him to act like that? To speak like that? He rested his forehead on the mirror. That's not how he behaved, or how he wanted to behave. It was all Ava. He had felt out of whack since he had met her two weeks ago in the coffee place. She had seen through his carefully constructed persona—the serious successful businessman—and pulled it apart bit by bit. He didn't like it; it made him feel exposed. No, that wasn't true. Quite the opposite. With her, he didn't have to pretend because she didn't allow him. With her, he felt like he could release a breath he didn't know he was holding. With her... he straightened up and got dressed. It was late. He could probably have put on his pajamas, but instead, he put on a suit. He needed to regain some control, to re-paint his persona. As soon as he was ready, he felt stupid. She'd look at him dressed like that and she'd know immediately what was going through his head. Her. That's what was going through his head. He grabbed his wallet and phone and left the house. He needed a long drive.

* * *

WHEN FACED with a moment of such an intense emotional intensity, Liam did what any mature man would do and the next day he avoided Ava at all costs. He buried himself in his work and nobody noticed the change. That's what New Liam did, right? Well, nobody noticed except Ava, but his withdrawal only seemed to confirm her view of the world and love, so she kept on with her life as if nothing strange had happened. Ava had faced big rejections in her life and had always become stronger for it. She thought she was immune to it by now. However, if she were to be honest with herself —and she always tried to be—this time she couldn't help but admit that it bothered her more than usual. Because of her attitude, most people assumed Ava was quick to decide at all times, but they'd be surprised to discover she was actually quite prone to introspection. Having lived on her own since she was a teenager, she'd had plenty of time to cultivate it. She wasn't expecting Liam to leave Scarlett for a two weeks crush on Ava—that's one of the things that she admired about him—but she hoped they could have remained friends. That would be impossible if he kept avoiding her. Well, too bad for him because when Ava didn't like a situation, she fixed it.

15 days with Ava

Ava intercepted Liam when he came back from work. He was loosening his tie, his feet barely inside the house, when she planted herself in front of him, feet apart and hands on her hips in a superhero pose. He jumped back and cleared his throat.

"Hey, good afternoon," he said.

"You're avoiding me," she replied.

He looked around, checking nobody could hear them.

"Can we talk somewhere else?" She relaxed her stance and smiled.

"Sure, where?"

He looked around again and his shoulders drooped as if he was suddenly exhausted.

* * *

HE CLOSED the door to the library but didn't turn around. He just looked over his shoulder at her. She had sat down and stretched out her legs, her hands over her belly, completely at ease. It rankled him that she was so calm. He couldn't stay still and he hated himself for it. He wanted to be as composed as her.

"Did you have to come to me like that just as I got in?" he growled.

"I figured you'd be stupid enough to feel awkward after what we spoke yesterday and wanted to clear the air."

"By calling me stupid?"

"Nothing has changed, you know?" That made him turn around. "If it makes you feel better, we can pretend it never happened."

"It should make me feel better," he muttered, turning his back to her again. He wandered over to his desk and picked up a stapler. He started fiddling with it.

"We're friends," she said. "I'd like to stay friends with you for a long time, but I can't if you avoid me."

He flopped down onto a chair—he really couldn't stay still—and rubbed his nose. "I want to be friends too."

"Great. That's all cleared then. I really want to laugh with someone at the next party. Liv is way too nice to let me make fun of people, but you are even worse than me." He laughed softly.

"I take exception to that. You are by far worse than me."

"Maybe I am, but I can't help it. I'll strive to be better." They smiled at each other.

"Thank you for talking to me," he said. "I really was being stupid."

"I know, but if it makes you feel better, I really thought I was going to have to kick your ass to make you change, but you always listen. It's really annoying."

"As you said, I'll strive to do better next time and ignore you completely." He stood up and together they headed for the door.

"I really hope you do," she said.

"Because you'd like to kick my ass sometime?" he ventured as he opened the door.

"See? Annoying. Stop listening to what I say."

"OK, then I'll call the dealer to cancel that appointment to look at electric cars." She whipped around, her smile gone.

"Don't you dare." He laughed and run out the door before she could kick his ass for real.

* * *

LIAM THOUGHT he'd had a great idea in the library. It was something innocent, something they could do together as friends. They were visiting during the day, with plenty of people around. It wouldn't be awkward. Right? He really needed to get his shit together. If he had thought for one minute about it, he would have realized it was going to be a nightmare. As soon as they arrived at the dealership, everybody assumed she was his girlfriend or, worse, his wife. Why did everyone at the dealer feel the need to greet them both and call her Mrs. Stewart? Ava laughed the first time and teased him mercilessly about it. "Honey," she said, "thank you so much for getting me a car." She then told the dealer that she'd had a terrible haircut that week, and this was Liam's way of making her feel better. It made him sound so posh. He bet the story would circulate all around the dealership by the end of the day. However, by the third time someone had confused them for a couple, even Ava was tiring. They replied at the same time, "We're just friends." They might have sounded harsher than they intended because the dealer was visibly taken aback. Liam just wanted to finish that appointment without ending thoroughly humiliated.

That dealership specialized in electric cars. Ava looked at the rows and rows of cars with a twinkle in her eyes. She broke into a run when she saw the latest model of V-Cars, the leading brand in electric cars.

"Liam!" she shouted at him to hurry. "This is the inteli9. Its kinetic recharger it's so advanced that it can replenish half the battery if you let it down a hill for thirty minutes. Combined with the long-life battery, it can run for double the time of the previous model. I just want to open its engine and pull it apart." Liam wasn't looking at the car. He was looking at Ava, a half-smile on his lips. She didn't notice, completely absorbed in the car. "You need to try it. This is The Car, Liam. How I wish I could work on the kinetic charger. Do you think I could make it recharge infinitely? It would be a completely green car, totally self-sufficient."

Liam asked the dealer for a test run and handed the keys to Ava. She looked at them as a child when you give them a new toy. Liam sat down on the back seat and let Ava ask the dealer all the questions she had cramming her head. They went for a half an hour ride and Ava didn't stop smiling for even a second. Whenever she maneuver she'd say 'Look how smooth it moves." She'd also repeatedly look at the dash-board and comment on the consumption. "The numbers barely move, look," she said, half turning her face to Liam. "It barely uses any energy." When they returned to the dealer-ship, the dealer left them alone in the car to discuss it. Liam moved to the passenger seat at the front. Ava run her hands through the steering wheel.

"It's as good as I imagined. Did you see how effortlessly it moved? And it shows in the display how much energy is consumed and how much it has recharged."

"You might have mentioned it during the ride," he replied with a smile. For the first time since he'd known her, he saw her blush, and it nearly took his breath away.

"Sorry," she replied. She laid her head on the wheel. "Can humans marry cars already? It should totally be allowed." He covered his mouth with his hand and smothered a laugh. "Sorry again, I'm getting carried away," she said, not in the least sorry.

"Have you decided?" the dealer asked.

"We're taking it," Liam said. Ava clutched his arm and asked if he was serious. "You said it's the best there is. I trust your opinion," he said.

"You need to let me borrow it, please." She looked at him with puppy dog eyes. He covered her face with his hand and playfully pushed her away.

"Of course, I will. You'll steal it otherwise."

Perhaps in the end it hadn't been such a bad idea. By the time they left the dealership, they were talking and laughing together, all awkwardness forgotten.

* * *

ON THE WAY HOME, Ava's phone rang. She took it out of her pocket and looked at the screen. Liam couldn't help it and looked at her phone from the corner of his eyes. The display showed it was Lewis. Liam's hands went white as he grabbed the steering wheel with too much force.

"Hey, what's up?" Ava said on the phone. Did she sound happy or uncomfortable? Liam couldn't tell, not that he could ever tell what she was thinking. She might say everything that she wants, but Liam never knew when she was being serious. "Tonight? I can't, sorry. I already have plans. Have fun though." Liam tried to think if Ava had any plans tonight or if she was making an excuse. He stopped himself. He shouldn't be thinking about that at all. It was nothing—it should be nothing—to him if she saw other people. Lewis was saying something, but Liam couldn't hear it. It was long though. Why wouldn't he shut up? Ava had already said she was busy. Some people are too clingy, Liam decided. Ava laughed and Liam felt like a rock had lodged itself in his stomach. "I know exactly what you mean," Ava said. She tucked some hair behind her ear. Was that a sign of flirting? Was Ava flirting on the phone?

A car honked behind Liam as he stopped abruptly and parked. The car passed them and glared at Liam. Ava looked at him in confusion and he mouthed the word 'coffee' as he pointed at the coffee shop on the other side of the street. Ava mouthed back 'decaf'. He gave her a thumbs up and crossed the street. The place was empty, and they greeted him as he came in. He picked up a menu and read it while standing near the entrance. From time to time he looked through the window at his car, checking if Ava was still on the phone. When she took the phone away from her ear, Liam moved quickly to the counter and ordered two coffees to take away.

He climbed into the car and handed Ava her decaf. She thanked him with a smile. He put his coffee in the cup holder and drove off.

"Can you drop me near the station?" Ava asked him.

"I thought you were going home," he said.

"I was, but there's been a change of plans."

Liam turned right to take her to the station. When they arrived, she stepped out of the car, gave him a little wave, and entered the station. Liam couldn't see if there was someone waiting for her inside or not. It bothered him. And it bothered him he had no right to be bothered.

* * *

AVA RETURNED to the house a couple of hours later. There was a little handcrafts shop behind the station and she had wanted to pick up a present for Liv. When they had been making the necklaces, she noticed she was using kitchen scissors to cut the strings. Ava got her a new pair of small ones with the shape of a heron that came in a pretty case. She hoped she liked it.

Ava heard a noise coming from one of the bathrooms upstairs and she knocked on the door to check if Liv was inside, while calling her name. Instead of a reply, she heard a lot of noise inside, as if something had been dropped and while trying to pick it up, they had knocked down more things. Ava smiled, convinced it was Liv and thinking of ways to tease her. After a full couple of minutes, the door opened and Scarlett came out in such a rush that she almost knocked down Ava. Both women were almost the same height, but Scarlett was thinner and more fragile, and Ava stabilized her by holding her upper arms.

"Wow, is everything alright? You don't look too well," Ava said. Scarlett took a couple of steps back, her head looking down. Ava grew worried she was going to be sick, so she got closer to her and kept her hands hovering around the other woman, in case she fell. "Do you need to lie down?" Scarlett mumbled a "No, thanks" and walked around Ava, but instead of going into Liam's room, she headed towards the stairs. "I'll help you," Ava insisted. Scarlett paused on the stairs and half turned. Still looking down, she repeated there was no need, but this time Ava caught something new in her voice. Scarlett wasn't sick, she was crying.

Ava knew that convention dictates that when someone cries you leave them alone, as most people consider crying in public something shameful. However, there is a difference between crying at home and doing it in your boyfriend's bathroom. This meant that something bad had happened unexpectedly and that you didn't want to tell your partner about it—or your partner had made you cry. Ava wasn't going to let her go away without offering her help once more. She joined Scarlett on the stairs and asked her to follow her. Like most people, Scarlett didn't even question her and just walked after her. Ava led them to her room and closed the door behind them.

"You can rest for a while here," she said. Scarlett went into Ava's en-suite bathroom and turned on the tap to wash her face. Ava sat down on her bed. "Scarlett, I know we haven't spoken a lot, but if you need anything, I'm here for you." The only reply was the running water. She leaned on the bedframe and waited. The tap closed and Scarlett's heels could be heard moving inside the bathroom. "I have some makeup you can use to retouch your eyes," Ava added. Scarlett came out looking more composed and offered a small smile to Ava. She hovered at the bathroom door.

"Thanks," she said, her voice small and rough.

"Everything alright?"

"Yes. I think I'll take a cab. If Liam asks, can you tell him I wasn't feeling well? I'll text him from home, but I can't... Sorry to put you in this position."

"No need to apologize. I'll take care of everything here. You go have some rest." Scarlett adjusted her bag on her shoulder and headed towards the room door. "But Scarlett, I know we're not that close, but you should probably talk to someone about it. Someone that will understand." Scarlett stopped with the hand on the door handle.

"And if I don't understand it myself?"

"All the more reason to. Sometimes understanding our own emotions is harder than others." Scarlett laughed softly, although there was no humor in it.

"I don't know. I find it damn hard to know what others are thinking most of the time." She sighed and squared her shoulders, readying herself to go downstairs again. Without realizing it, Ava had left her bed and was now standing closer to her.

"There is one thing that you can know for sure: whatever you're feeling or thinking, someone has felt it before.

Emotions are complicated, but for better or worse, they're also universal. You might not get clarity, but you can get understanding."

Scarlett nodded, both in agreement and thanks, but she hesitated before leaving the room.

"Please," she said, "don't tell Liam about, you know, how you found me." Ava promised her to keep her secret and Scarlett left the room.

As she saw Scarlett leaving, Ava was thinking she had a pretty good idea of what was going through the other woman's head. It's a shame she was absolutely wrong.

16 days with Ava

A va and Nova went in together into the lawyer's office. After the last investor's fiasco, Nova wanted to make sure everything was correct. She didn't have a lawyer on retainer, but his brother had recommended her to use this one. She had done some work for his company and her rates were affordable. Ava had, of course, her own lawyer, but Liam had told Nova that it was standard procedure for both sides to get everything checked and Ava didn't even question Nova's request to come with her. Nova would never tell this to her brother, but she felt out of her depth in the legal area. She was thankful to have Ava with her, even if it was to look at her contract through the microscope.

They spent almost two hours there, but they left with a seal of approval on the contract—also with an invoice that gave Nova cold sweats. She'd have to talk to Liam about what could be described as affordable. She could pay it, of course, all thanks to Ava's investment, but she wasn't used to these sums of money. One thing that Nova liked about Ava is that she was never patronizing with her. She didn't know if it was because she had also started a company as a young woman or if it was just her personality, but it made Nova feel as if they were on an equal footing. During the meeting, she had treated Nova as, well, as a business partner. Nova felt giddy.

"I'll buy you lunch," Nova said. "Actually, I'll buy you lunch, dinner, and breakfast from today for the rest of your life."

"I'm not sure I want to be in business with someone that spends her money so carelessly," she replied. "I'll accept one lunch, though."

Nova and Ava had gotten along from the moment they met, but they were discovering a new aspect of their friendship. Nova had spoken about her business before with friends, but they understood little about it and it had been always a bit of a one-sided conversation. With Ava, she could talk for hours. And talk they did. They subtly kicked them out of the restaurant—with the classic move of leaving the bill on the table—and they moved to a nearby cafe. It was getting dark, and they were still at it. It was almost dinnertime when they both got a text from Liv asking where they were. Ava's face lit up and typed furiously an answer. "*Come over, we need you,*" it said.

"Your sister was a machine for financial plans in college. She can help us with the year five projection. I think that if we increase the commission by 1% we can accelerate growth, but I'd like her to check the maths."

Nova crossed her arms and rubbed them with her hands.

"She's busy with wedding stuff. I don't want to bother her."

"Nonsense. That wedding doesn't need more planning. And she'll love to help you."

Nova played with the spoon in her cup, swirling it inside the now empty cup.

"I know what you're doing, you know?" Nova said. Tiny wrinkles appeared around Ava's eyes. "About Liv and the wedding. And Liam and the wedding…" she trailed off. Ava opened her mouth to speak, but Nova didn't let her. "I've seen how Liam looks at you, how he searches for you in every room, and how he tries to see your reaction to everything he says." Ava took a deep breath.

"I'm leaving in two weeks," she said. Nova flinched.

"That's not what I meant. I'm trying to say that the change I've seen in him—"

"Nova," Ava interrupted, "I won't harm your family or Scarlett. Ever. I know when it's my time to leave, and I promise I will. And give your brother a little credit. He loves your family too much to do anything bad." Nova bent over the table and grasped Ava's forearm.

"That's not what I meant. I actually —" But Ava had turned towards the door where Liv was waving at them. She sat down at their table and took off her coat.

"I did not know you were so close by," she said, slightly out of breath. "Are we staying or moving somewhere else? I need something to drink."

* * *

AVA DUG out of her bag the projections for Nova's business and explained to Liv the ideas that she and Nova had been discussing that afternoon. Liv took a pen and started to do some numbers on the back of one paper. She had always had a head for numbers. Ava was happy to see her friend like that. Liv was a pretty girl, gentle and kind, and some people forgot what a ferocious brain she had behind that facade. Now, looking at her explaining to her sister what she would change in her projections, it was as if she had transformed into another person. She came alive. Nova and Liv forgot Ava was there, both completely absorbed in the discussion. Both looked in that moment like their older brother, with an air of confidence the world couldn't help but take notice. Ava excused herself to make a phone call, although she could have easily had stepped out without them noticing. And that's how it should be, she thought. She sat outside on a bench right next to the cafe and replied to some of her pending emails. She made some phone calls too—she hadn't lied about that. Suddenly, Nova came out of the cafe and waved goodbye at her.

"I'm late to meet with some friends," she shouted as she run towards the bus stop. "See you at home." Ava waved back and returned to the cafe to collect Liv.

"That was fun," Liv said as she turned on the car. "I hadn't seen Nova's business plan. She's got a solid model there."

"It reminded me of college," Ava said. "I've never seen someone as happy as you while calculating profit and losses."

"Hey, many people find it fascinating."

"Your sister is not one of them, though, but she doesn't need to. She might not be good at that, but she has a very strategic mind. Perhaps someone can help her do that part." Liv looked down with a guilty face. She had been so caught up with the wedding that she had ignored Nova completely. She wasn't sure why she had become so obsessed with it, but she felt that there was something not quite right. Liv had gone through all the arrangements many times—and so had Liam—but she knew that there was something that was going to go wrong on the day. She just couldn't figure out what it was. She promised herself to help Nova once the wedding was over. Actually... they were leaving on their honeymoon right after the wedding. But once she was back from the honeymoon, eventually, at some point, she was going to help Nova.

17 days with Ava

A small bell at the top of the door rang as Ava stepped into the bridal shop, Liv following behind. A woman in a pale blue suit came from the back of the store and welcomed them with the whitest teeth that can realistically be achieved. She recognized Liv immediately—when someone buys a dress as expensive as Liv's, you never forget her face—and ushered them into a room. The shop owner brought some coffee for both of them before going to the back of the store to grab Liv's dress. She returned with it and directed Liv to the changing room. Ava sipped her coffee in silence until Liv came out. She stepped out of the changing room in a pearl white satin dress. It was simple, but it hugged her body like a second skin and had a deep plunge in the back that made it more daring. Ava thought nothing could have been more perfect for her friend.

"I wouldn't make any more adjustments. What do you think?" the consultant asked.

Liv stared at her reflection with a look that none of the two other women could read. The consultant didn't show it, but she was panicking, thinking that she was about to have a Bridezilla moment where Liv wanted to change the dress last minute. She had always thought the dress was a bit too plain for what was going to be the wedding of the year in their town, but Liv looked entirely convinced when she chose it. She started to mentally catalog the dresses they had in the store that could fit her off the rack.

Ava stood next to her Liv and cocked her head to the side, looking at her friend in the mirror.

"Liv?" she asked. Liv run her hands through the silky material. "A penny for your thoughts?"

"I was just thinking… never mind."

"Is it feeling too real?" Ava offered tentatively. Liv shook her head.

"No, it still doesn't. Am I really getting married?" To the consultant, she asked, "Is this normal?" The consultant gave an inward sigh of relief and kept her professional smile.

"Of course it is. Some people go through the whole ceremony with a feeling of unreality. It's a lot to take in."

Liv was still looking at her reflection in the mirror. Ava knew that her friend tended to bottle up her feelings. It came from a misguided perception that her friends would be bothered if they had to listen to her complaints. She also knew that pressuring her to open up wasn't the best strategy, it required a different approach.

"It's not the dress," Ava said. The consultant lost her smile for a moment.

"But she looks stunning in it," she replied. Both friends ignored the worker.

"I know," Liv replied. "It's not it."

"I... I'm not sure we'll be able to find another dress last minute," the consultant said, trying to not show her internal turmoil.

"Let's go for a coffee," Ava said.

"No, no," Liv replied. "There's no need."

"Perhaps coffee is a good idea. It'll help you clear your mind. You can try the dress again and see it anew," the consultant said.

"The dress is perfect," Liv said.

"Is it?" the consultant asked.

Ava popped her head from the other side of Liv.

"Darling, she loves the dress. That's not the issue."

This time, the consultant couldn't contain her relieved breath. Right after, she realized what the two women were saying. Oh, shit.

"I'm not getting cold feet," Liv said, a bit too loud.

"I know," Ava replied.

"The feeling will pass. It's normal," the consultant said.

"I'm going to sell my company," Ava said.

"What?" the other two women asked, one in confusion and the other in disbelief. Liv gathered the train of her dress and stepped down from the raised area. "Ava," she said, "that company is your baby."

"I just need a change."

"Where is this coming from?"

"What can I say? Maybe it's in my blood, leaving my babies behind." Liv grabbed Ava's forearm gently and steered her toward the sofa. The consultant followed them, asking Liv not to sit on the dress. Liv just waved her away. That showed how upset she was, otherwise she'd never have been that rude to someone. "Don't get all stressed out, Liv. I'm going to make tons of money from selling it. Like an absurd amount of money."

"You didn't create that company for money. You wanted to make electric cars the norm, to make a difference."

Ava crossed her legs and laid back on the sofa.

"My dear, most people walk away from things often, almost daily, and nobody thinks badly of them for it."

"I'm not getting cold feet," Liv said with some annoyance.

"And I think I'm not the best fit for the company anymore."

Liv grabbed her hand and rubbed it. "Are you sure it's not a phase?"

"There's something that doesn't feel right anymore and this is the type of life path that you have to be 100% sure about before you commit further."

"Ava, most people are never 100% sure of anything. They just choose the path they want to pursue and stick to it. There'll always be some doubts, but they choose to stay."

Both friends looked at each other, thinking about entirely different things.

"We, my friend, were raised very differently," Ava concluded. Liv smiled and stood up, smoothing inexistent wrinkles from her dress. Both knew that the conversation wasn't over.

* * *

IT WAS safe to say that by this point, all the Stewart siblings were fed up with parties and social engagements. They weren't used to so many late nights anymore, and they all had too much going through their minds. But it was a party organized by Mason's parents, so they couldn't really say no to it. They all looked beautiful, but their smiles didn't quite reach their eyes.

Ava, on the other hand, looked like someone on her first day of holidays. She was surrounded by three older couples, all of them laughing already at her jokes. A woman asked her if she was single to introduce her to her son. She took her phone and showed Ava a picture of him. Ava whistled and made a comment that had them all in stitches and the other woman puffing up in pride.

Liam was standing behind Ava, back to back, in another circle of people, and heard it all. He was so distracted he missed half of the conversation happening in front of him. He excused himself and left the room. Liam needed a drink, and he needed to be far away from Ava. He reminded himself he only had to endure this agony for another fourteen days and then she'd be gone. He abandoned the full glass on the table and went to get some air.

* * *

LIV WAS HOLDING Mason's arm, right next to his parents, as they introduced her to some of their friends. She could feel Mason's restless energy through their linked arms. He hated this kind of social function where everything was too formal. She squeezed his arm and whispered.

"Just a few minutes and they'll leave us alone," she said. He got close to her ear.

"And then we can escape this horror?"

"Your parents organized this in our honor. We can't leave." Something crossed his face. He'd had an idea. Liv was always wary of Mason's ideas when he was bored.

"Liv, my love, aren't you tired?" he said. "Maybe we can rest a bit in my room." She tensed.

"I'm not having a quickie while they're throwing a party for us outside the door." He pursed his lips, but let it go. Mason waved to a passing waiter and grabbed two glasses. Liv extended a hand, but he didn't pass her any glass. He was drinking both himself. If she wasn't on board with his idea, he was going to get drunk instead. Liv checked her watch. It was going to be a long night.

* * *

Nova was looking at her phone in a corner of the house when she saw her brother pass by. He didn't even glance in her direction. His strides were long and his face determined. He opened the glass doors leading to the garden and stepped outside. He inhaled deeply as if he had been drowning inside.

"The party is going well, I see," Nova said from behind Liam. He looked towards her and his lips quirked to the side.

"If you pretend to be sick, I'll take you home," he replied.

"And leave poor Liv alone?"

"Ava is in there," he said. Nova thought he detected a hint of annoyance in his voice. He saw the phone in her hand. The screen was lit up. He smiled. "Checking your emails at a party? Like a true entrepreneur." Nova looked at the screen and locked the phone.

"Do you think so?"

"What?"

"That I look like an entrepreneur?"

"You don't look like one, sis. You are one." She smiled, but it disappeared quickly.

"What if it doesn't go well?"

"Then it doesn't." He shrugged. "This isn't a test. Nobody will fail you if you don't make it. You pick yourself up and find something new to do."

She got closer to her brother and hugged him from the back.

"I want this so much, Liam. Have you ever felt like you want something so deeply that it occupies all your waking moments? Even your dreams?"

Liam looked back at the house. He could see the party raging on through the windows.

"Yes, I've had," he replied softly.

"And how do you deal with it?"

"I don't know." He stood a few seconds more looking in, watching Ava move around the party. The way she tip back her head when she laughed, or to the side when she was paying attention. How her fingers drummed on her glass when she wanted to say something. Her eyes, just the way they expressed her every emotion. And then, just for a second, how her eyes scanned the room, and she frowned. She was looking for him. Liam didn't know that your heart could expand and drop to the pit of your stomach at the same time. He knew then that she wasn't as unaffected as she seemed. He marveled at it, at her. If she could be so strong, then so could he. For her, for himself, for the hope of one day being friends as they promised to be. He steeled himself, turned around, and draped an arm around Nova's shoulder.

"Enough of a break. Let's mingle."

HE CAME BACK into the room as if someone had flipped a switch. All traces of exhaustion had vanished. He was at his most charming. He was the man of the multi-billion dollars company with a handshake that could crush your hand. The man that could make you smile or cry with the lift of an eyebrow. He was powerful, and he was in control. He drew attention without meaning to. People would come over to talk to him, the tall handsome man that exuded confidence. Liam talked to all of them. He memorized all their names. He was engaged in the conversation and always had something interesting to add. What an impressive man, someone whispered, but he still heard. He saw his reflection in the window and he didn't recognize himself.

* * *

PEOPLE WOULD HAVE BEEN SURPRISED to discover that Ava was thoroughly and utterly exhausted. It wasn't because the party had been boring. She had met some interesting people, and she never found herself without someone to talk to, but she hadn't been feeling as energetic as she looked. When she arrived at the party, she had been genuinely excited. She loved meeting fresh faces and making friends, but at some point, she had discovered Liam looking at her. His eyes were filled with such a sense of sadness that she nearly run to him and hugged him. But she couldn't do it. Not in front of so many people, and not when they were alone. So she did what was best for both of them. She had become even more open and sociable with everyone else. He had to see her happy and unconcerned. He had to believe that this was easy for her, that she'd forget him and move on. So he could move on. And then she saw him change. He became the life of the party. He always had at least four people surrounding him, listening to something he said, preening when he asked them a question. They were basking in his attention, the powerful thing that it was. The same woman that had shown her the picture of her son was looking at Liam and unconsciously biting her lip. However, maybe other people couldn't tell, but Ava could see the truth. His posture was too stiff, and his smile smaller than it usually was. He would ask one question from each person in the group as an automatic thing. And she wondered… she wondered what it would be like if she had been more selfish; if that day in the kitchen she had closed the gap between them. Maybe then this tightness, like a rope pulling at them waiting to snap and let them fall, wouldn't exist. Maybe then he'd be smiling for real and his shoulders would relax, leaning towards her. She turned towards the table with drinks and left her glass on the table as if those treacherous thoughts would stay on the table as well. Ava believed people made problems for themselves and this, Liam and her, would be the definition of it. She didn't need his guilty eyes the morning after when he'd realized that he'd hurt Scarlett. She didn't need to watch him leave, like every other person in her life. By the time she turned away from the table, she had wiped all thoughts of Liam from her head.

* * *

AVA ALSO HAD Liv to consider. Her friend looked stressed. She saw her swapping Mason's drinks for water, and pushing away waiters that were offering him a refill. She joined her friend and helped her curve Mason's thirst. Near the end of the party, however, Mason grabbed Liv's waist and started a slow dance with her. Ava could hear sweet words coming from him.

"You're the best, babes," he whispered to her. "I have the most beautiful woman in the room with me. I don't deserve you, and I love you, babes." Liv's nervousness seemed to evaporate at his words. She grinned and fixed her eyes on Mason's face.

It amazed Ava how complex people were. Despite all of Mason's flaws, Liv seemed to love him deeply. She believed Mason loved Liv as well, but she also knew his definition of love might not match hers. As she saw them twirl around the room, she hoped Liv never found that out.

* * *

AS AVA, Liam and Nova made their way outside, people stopped them constantly to say goodbye to them. Between Ava and Liam, they had spoken to the entire party—and charmed them, too. Someone passed behind them, trying to squeeze back into the party, bumping into Liam and making him lose his balance. Ava grabbed him by the waist and helped him stay upright. Liam regained his footing but didn't move from Ava's arms. They both stared at each other's eyes.

"I've just saved your life," Ava said. She was smiling softly at him, her hands holding him close. He tucked a loose strand behind her ear and then dropped his eyes to her lips. He stepped even closer to her. Her smile faltered and release him. He grabbed her wrist and stilled. "Liam…" she said. He put one of her arms on his shoulder and held the other in his hand. He then grabbed her waist with his free hand.

"We haven't danced at all tonight, you and I." His face was calm. His mouth quirked in a half-smile and his eyes never left hers.

"I thought we were leaving," she said. He shrugged.

"Since when do you care about those things?" They moved to the rhythm of the music, the rest of the party forgotten. A small space cleared around them, but they were largely ignored. Only Nova looked at them with a pained expression. He made a full circle, her swinging in his arms, and she giggled. The sound was strangely girlish coming from her. As the song slowed down, so did they, until they swayed lightly on the same spot. Too soon, the song ended, and they parted. They were both slightly out of breath, even though it had been a slow dance.

"I had to do it one time. One damn time," he said. She nodded.

"Let's go," she replied.

Near the door, they said goodbye to Liv. Mason was hugging her from behind, nudging her ear with his nose. She smiled sweetly at him. Her family and Ava kissed her goodbye and called a taxi to get them home.

On the drive back, Nova was dozing off with her head on

Liam's shoulder. Ava was sitting at the front, chatting quietly with the driver so they didn't wake up Nova. Liam watched her eyes move expressively from the rearview mirror, the way they wrinkled when she smiled or got bigger when she got excited. Two weeks, he reminded himself. Two weeks of torture. Two weeks left to enjoy his time with her.

Ava was having her morning coffee when Liv came into the room. She had under-eye bags and her pupils looked red.

"What's wrong?" Ava asked. "You look like you haven't slept a wink. Did Mason keep you up all night?" Liv shrugged her shoulders and stirred her coffee.

"The party ended late, and I was way too excited afterward to go to bed," she replied. Ava observed her friend with half hooded eyes. She finally shook her head.

"I don't think that's it," she said. "You look like that one time you caught Megan cheating on Sam and didn't know what to do. It's your *I'm completely lost* look." Liv tried for levity and laughed lightly, but Ava didn't fall for it. Liv saw Ava hadn't laughed with her and looked down at her coffee again.

"I'm fine, I swear."

"I'm here for you, you know that, don't you?" Liv raised her cup to her lips, but her hand trembled and she lowered it. Ava waited for her friend to speak. However, when it was obvious she wasn't going to say anything, Ava stood up and went to pour herself another coffee from the machine on the side table.

"Is it money?" Ava asked while she put the tiny capsule on the coffee machine. Still, Liv said nothing. "Then it's love," she continued with a sigh. "What did Mason do? I'll kick his ass."

"God, Ava, why do you have to try to fix everyone all the time? Sometimes people only want to be left alone," Liv said. She had raised her voice, and she covered her mouth right after. Ava took the freshly poured cup and sat right next to her friend.

"I can count with one hand the number of times you've shouted at someone in your life, and I'd still have enough fingers to hold this cup. I'm not trying to fix anyone, I'm just offering a sympathetic ear."

"It's nothing," Liv said. "I just... Mason... I feel uncomfortable about something, but it's me just being silly." She risked another glance at Ava, who was watching her intently. "Mason likes to play pranks on people, and he played one on me. I didn't like him and told him so. Happy?"

Ava licked her lips and didn't say anything for a few seconds.

"What was the prank?"

"It's over, just let it be." Ava leaned forward.

"Whatever you tell me right now, I won't ever repeat it. I'm serious, Liv, not a single comment. Not a glance at you when something reminds me of it. I won't even think about it. But something tells me you're downplaying this. I'll just listen. I promise."

Liv's head was almost touching the rim of her cup and one of her hands stirred the spoon slowly. She took a deep breath.

"Yesterday after the party ended, Mason and I went upstairs and he—" Ava held still, leaving Liv space to find her words, but the hand holding the coffee mug was so tight it was white. "After we did it, he took his phone and showed me something on the screen. He had filmed us doing it. He laughed and kept playing it. I—I got upset with him, which was the wrong move. Mason doesn't respond well when you confront him like that. But I calmed him down and he explained to me it was just for the two of us, as a memory of that night. In a twisted kind of way, it was sweet of him, I guess? I just don't like the idea of me somewhere in a video like that. What if his phone gets stolen or hacked? I'm not mad at him, but I just don't like it very much, but I'm sure I'm overreacting."

Ava knew since she was a child that she had a terrible temper, but she had learned early on how to control it. Looking at her, nobody would be able to tell how furious she was, not even her best friend. This time, however, she was struggling to rein it in. She wanted to drive to Mason's house and rip his throat out. Or even better, some other parts of his anatomy. She instead took two deep breaths.

"My dear Liv, if you don't like that video being out there, ask him to delete it. If he loves you, he'll understand and do so. I know you have issues confronting people and making your needs heard, but you know deep down that what he did is wrong, or you wouldn't lose sleep over it."

"What if he gets mad at me? What if he breaks up with me?" she said. "We have the wedding in a week and…"

"Why would he get mad?" Ava asked, but at Liv's face, she continued. "He was angry yesterday when you weren't happy about the video?" Tears started to fall down Liv's face, and she tried to wipe them away. Ava clasped her hand.

"Listen Liv, you have the power here. He did something illegal, without your consent. You have nothing to cry about. Call him this instant, tell him to delete that video or you'll drag his ass to court. Do you hear me?"

"What if he uploads the video instead? I'd die of embarrassment."

"He's in that video, too. Why should you feel ashamed and not him? If the world sees that video, they'll only see how he abused your confidence and what a tiny dick he has."

"I can't, Ava, I can't." Liv cried in earnest now.

"Tell me something, Liv, just between us. I already promised nothing you say here today will ever be repeated. What do you want to happen?" Liv hiccuped.

"I want that video gone," she replied.

"And what about the marriage? If it weren't so near it, would you stop it?" Liv looked up at her friend. Unshed tears pooled in her eyes and her cheeks glistened from the ones she had already shed. She covered her nose with the cuff of her shirt. However, despite her tears, her eyes looked determined when she spoke.

"I should have never said yes."

Ava knew they had to do something about that video, but Liv was too overwhelmed at that moment to act. Ava also knew that Liv's disposition was way too gentle to confront something like this. She wasn't like that, but she understood enough about human nature to know that most people were like Liv and that the world was a better place thanks to those with a softer personality. Luckily for Liv, her friend had no problems facing a good fight and, unfortunately for Mason, she was feeling murderous.

* * *

THAT NIGHT AVA parked a couple of houses down Mason's, waiting for him to come home. The moment his car pulled into the street, she recognized it immediately. That color... She stayed in her borrowed car until he went into his house and then walked to his door. As she passed by, she noticed his car was squeaky clean. "I bet he washes it himself," she muttered to herself. Ava loved cars as much as anyone, but she failed to understand how someone could use them as a sign of identity. Men complained about women using fashion for that same purpose all the time, and yet a car was way more expensive. For her, cars were engineering master-pieces, built for efficiency. When she saw the flashy tires Mason had installed, she made a mental note to make effi-cient tires her next project. But first, her first project: murdering Mason. Just kidding, she'd settle for making him sweat.

She rang the bell and waited. When he opened the door, half-naked, she had plastered on her face an ear-to-ear smile. From an objective perspective, Ava could appreciate he was a handsome man. She could understand what her friend had seen in him at first. What she had trouble understanding is how Liv had stayed with him after a one-night stand. He was clearly confused why she was there, but he invited her in and offered her a drink. He guided her to his living room and went to the kitchen to get a drink.

"Does Liv know you're coming?" he said tentatively as he offered her a glass. He was smiling. He thought Ava was coming to seduce him, and he didn't look opposed to it. With an extreme effort, she kept her smile in place too.

"Can you please grab your phone?" she said. That clearly wasn't the answer he was expecting, but like most people, when asked directly for something, he complied. "Now you're going to unlock it, hand it over to me, and let me delete the video you took last night of you and Liv." He took two steps back and his face hardened.

"I don't know what you're talking about," he said.

"Then you won't mind me going through your photos to check."

"I do. I have private stuff here."

"I don't care about your porn or your trashy hookups. I just want to make sure Liv's video disappears completely."

He hesitated, then crossed his arms and pulled himself to his full height. He was a big man and he knew it. Ava was a tall woman, but he was even taller and could easily look at her from above. He puffed up his chest and flexed his muscles.

"And why do I need to do anything you say? Do you think you can get this phone from me? You're alone in my house. I can basically say—and do—whatever I want."

Ava kept smiling. He clearly wasn't expecting that. She put the glass on the table and sat down on the sofa. She spread her arms to the sides of the sofa and crossed her legs. "Let me explain to you in detail how I'm getting that phone. Consenting to have sex and be seen naked doesn't extend to filming, as the first is a private act and filming violates the assumption of privacy. Best case scenario, you'll be convicted of voyeurism, but if you have shared it with anyone or uploaded it anywhere, it can be considered a sexual offense and you can face jail time. I'm hoping you haven't been so inane as to make that video public, but even if you haven't and you refuse to delete it, let me tell you that I have a full PR agency under retinue and I can ask them for advice on how to spread wide and large that Mason Miller is nothing but a little perverted voyeur." Mason's shoulders drooped slightly, but he seemed to realize and extended again to his full height. "But I won't stop there. Despite what you see in films and TV, women support other women. I'll personally call all the women in your known circle and explain to them what you have done. Next time you decide to use your little dick— no, Liv hasn't told me it's small, I could guess just by talking to you for five minutes—you'll be wondering if the woman you're with is going to take a photograph of it and share it around while we all laugh at you and your little manhood."

She stood and walked over to him. Suddenly, they looked almost the same height. "Now, what about you hand over your phone unlocked to me?"

"You're bluffing. Liv will never report me to the police."

"Gosh, you just get more tedious by the second. Everyone has a breaking point, Mason, and you found Liv's. I really don't have the time to hear you, little Mason. Your phone or the police?" His eyes flared red, but he still took his phone from his pocket and gave it to her. She smiled and thanked him. She typed a few things on the screen to remove the screen lock password and put it in her pocket. From her other pocket, she took a bunch of hundred-dollar bills and put them on his coffee table.

"That money is to buy a new phone. I'm taking this one with me to make sure that the video is gone. Once I've checked it thoroughly, I'll be crushing it to dust. Don't worry about me using any of your other *private* stuff against you. Unlike you, I understand the concepts of privacy and trust, how breaking them can hurt people, and the legal implications of my actions. Also, I have no interest in talking, seeing, or hearing about you ever again. You might receive a call from Liv or her family to discuss the best way to call off the wedding. And next time you think that something like what you did is a laugh or that you won't hurt the other person, think about what I told you. Think about all the women of your acquaintance laughing at your dick picks. Maybe you'll be able to feel some empathy and one day you'll manage to have a healthy relationship with another woman."

As soon as Ava left, Mason took the glass she had left on the table and drank it in one gulp. Despite what that video had caused, he had genuinely wanted to marry Liv and he couldn't understand how all had unraveled so quickly. His first instinct was to call Liv and apologize to her. It wasn't the first time he had done something bad to her, but Liv would always forgive him. He knew she was incapable of not forgiving people. However, he couldn't call her because Ava had taken his phone, and he was sure they wouldn't let him see her anytime soon. Instead, he went to a bar to have a drink. He wasn't someone prone to introspection, but Ava's words kept replaying in his mind. First, it was words like jail and criminal offense. It scared him that if he tried to talk to Liv to win her back, they'd call the police. But the more he drank, the more he kept hearing the words hurt and trust. The sad truth is that Mason had never pondered any of that before. His friends always laughed at his pranks and the video had been that, a prank. He thought Liv would laugh at it, and that was it. Didn't Liv get it was meant as a joke? And if Ava followed on her thread and called all her female friends, would they also laugh or get mad like Liv? He was on the verge of a revelation. Unfortunately, he kept drinking to the point of blacking out and the next morning, when he woke up lying down at the entrance to his house, he could only remember that Ava had taken his phone. Would they let her see Liv today?

19 days with Ava

Liv was curled on the sofa, a blanket covering her despite the warmth of the day. Her eyes were swollen and red. She kept changing channels nervously. Ava came into the room and put a phone on the table in front of her, but Liv ignored her and continued staring at the TV.

"You'd like to have a look at that phone," Ava said. Liv dropped her gaze to the phone, but it took her a few seconds to realize what she was looking at. She jumped from the sofa and grabbed it.

"Why do you have it?"

"I talked to Mason and we agreed he'd delete everything, and to make sure it was done, he gave me his phone. I've spent the last hour checking and deleting the video from his phone, different cloud backups, and folders. You'll be happy to know he hasn't shared it with anyone."

"He gave you his phone?" Liv asked with incredulity.

"Liv, what he did to you is illegal. He could serve up to a two years' sentence for it. It was in his best interest to delete any proof."

"But he's my boyfriend, and I agreed to have sex with him," she replied.

"But you didn't consent to film it. You have a right to your privacy. My company lawyers gave us all a very thorough course in privacy for both corporations and individuals. Trust me, he would be in deep trouble if we take this to the police."

Liv stared at the phone, not quite believing it. She crossed the room and hugged her friend tight. She started to cry.

"I was so scared, Ava. I thought my life was ruined," she said between sobs and hiccups.

"Shhh, it's alright. Nobody will see that video now."

"Thank you! Thank you! I can never repay this. Never." Ava stepped away from her friend's hug and dried her face.

"You've suffered enough in the hands of that asshole. You don't have to see him ever again. Can you imagine being married to that troll? You got away just in time." Ava tidied up Liv's hair, which she hadn't bothered combing that morning.

"Oh, my God, the wedding."

"I'll call the wedding planner, but you better tell your family first. Talk to your brother and he'll help you break the news to the rest of the guests."

"He's going to be furious."

"Nonsense. He'll move heaven and earth for his two sisters. How anyone can feel intimidated by your brother is beyond me."

"That's because nobody intimidates you."

"I definitely feel intimidated, until I remind myself that when I allow them to intimidate me, they gain power over me. When I take away that power, there's nothing they can do to me. The only power your brother has over me is the capacity to make me laugh, even when he doesn't intend to do so. Although I'll admit that the day I saw him wearing tight jeans, he could have asked me to do anything to him. I mean, for him."

"Ava, he's my brother." Liv laughed as she said it. Ava was so happy to see her laugh again.

"You also look great in jeans, but this friendship is strictly platonic." Liv laughed again, but she stopped when she heard the front door opening and the decided steps from Liam. Ava gave her a gentle nudge towards the door.

"Come on, that's your cue. Go talk to him. As with most things in life, the more you delay it, the harder it'll be."

* * *

LIAM WAS REMOVING his suit jacket when Liv knocked on the open door to his room.

"Hey, sis, come in. How's your day been?" He then noticed her puffy eyes and rushed to her. "What's the matter? Is everything alright?" Liv didn't immediately respond, and he grew more worried. "Come on, Liv. Talk to me. Are you hurt? What is it?" Liv just shook his head and visibly gathered herself before speaking.

"I—I need to cancel the wedding," she said. His shoulders relaxed and he let go of Liv's arms.

"Did you and Mason fight?" he asked.

"In a way..." she replied.

"If you want to cancel the wedding, of course you can, but are you sure you won't regret it once you make up?"

"I'm never talking to him again," she replied.

"OK, OK." He loosened his tie and hung it with the jacked on the back of a chair. "I'll call the wedding planner and send out cancellations tomorrow."

"Ava is already talking to the wedding planner," Liv replied.

He stopped, and for a moment Liv thought he was going

to say something. She knew how he felt about Ava meddling in the wedding organization, but he didn't look angry. Liv couldn't interpret his look.

"Very well," he said. "I'll send some cancellations in person to my business partners and let the wedding planner deal with the rest. But Liv…" He approached his sister again. "Are you going to tell me what is going on? You know I never liked Mason, but for you to change your mind so abruptly, something bad must have happened. Please, let me help you."

"Can we just leave it like that?" Liam hugged her sister tight to his chest and stroked her back in soothing motions.

"It's done. I won't ask again. But remember, I'm here to help you." Liv burrowed her face in his chest, but she didn't cry. She inhaled deeply and relaxed in his arms.

"He did something horrible, something I can't forgive him." She noticed him clench, and she got tense in response. She grabbed him as if she was afraid he'd run after Mason right then. "But I don't want you to do anything irrational. You have a temper, Liam, and I don't want you getting in trouble for me. Is it enough to know that it's been taken care of?"

Liam continued to stroke her back, her hair, deep in thought. He could hear Ava's voice in his head, telling him again to just listen to her sister. "I don't need to fix this for her," he told himself. "I just need to be here for her."

"If I promise not to do anything, will you tell me what happened? Not knowing will kill me, Liv." She looked up to find that it was him who was crying. A single tear fell down his face. "It's just," he said, "I have all these horrible images going through my mind of what could have happened to you."

"OK," she whispered. "OK." She rested her head on his chest and he embraced her tight again. There, in the warmth of his body, she told him what happened. And she told him what Ava had done for her, how she had recovered the video, and how she was sure she was safe. It didn't take long, but both felt exhausted by the end. Liv had felt guilty since it happened. She felt like it was somehow her fault, that she had allowed it. She expected Liam to tell her to be more careful, that she should have never gone out with Mason, but he didn't. He kissed the top of her head and told her he was sorry.

"It wasn't your fault," she responded.

"Neither was yours." This time Liv cried.

Liv could feel in the tension of Liam's muscles, how angry he was. However, he was keeping his promise and just listened. She was so used to him telling her what to do that his silence was puzzling.

"Nothing to say?" she asked, unable to stay quiet any longer.

"You know I love you, sis, don't you?" His voice sounded rough.

"I love you too." They sat down on his bed, still hugging each other. She fell asleep in his arms. He carefully lowered her onto the bed and covered her with a blanket. There was something he needed to do urgently.

* * *

LIAM STRODE into the kitchen where Ava was spreading some butter on a piece of bread. She popped the bread into her mouth and pointed at some food in offering. He stopped by the kitchen aisle and opened his mouth, but no words came out. Ava wondered if he had ever seen him so at a loss for words before. His family and friends could have clarified for her it was indeed a rare occasion.

"It looks like this family has much to thank you for.

Again," he said. "How you got that… how you got Mason to delete everything… I want to kill him."

"I admit I was very tempted myself to bash his head against that ridiculous car of his, but for once I thought before acting. You'd be proud of my self-control, I'm sure." He was too overwhelmed by the whole situation to laugh at her joke. He walked around the kitchen aisle and grabbed her hand.

"If you ever need anything, and I mean anything, it's yours."

"Well, you bought the car of my dreams…" she said.

"It's yours."

"Liam, I'm only joking. You don't owe me anything. Liv is one of my best friends. I'd do anything for her."

"Very few people would do what you did for their friends," he said.

"You'd do that for a friend and more. I know you." Her hand suddenly fascinated him. He raised it and started to trace it with his other hand.

"Yes," he said, still caressing her hand, "you know me." Gently, he lowered her hand. "Which is why you know that I'm serious when I say that whatever you need—" She cut him off by covering his mouth with both her hands. He stopped.

"No debt, Liam. The things I do for those I love are always free."

Before he could respond, his phone started ringing. He cursed when he saw it was Scarlett calling. He had forgotten he was dining with her that night. Ava saw the name on the display too and offered Liam a smile that didn't quite reach her eyes.

"You need to go, don't you?" He didn't reply, just stared at his phone ringing incessantly.

"I feel like such a failure, Ava," he whispered. She took a

step forward and extended her hands towards him, but stopped before touching him.

"No, Liam—"

"I failed Nova and Liv, spectacularly. And I'm failing you and Scarlett."

"Stop it."

"But I—"

"No, stop right now," she told him firmly. "You haven't failed me." She grabbed his upper arms. "You and I, we never... We're friends. We'll be good friends." He looked deeply into her hazel eyes, as if the answer to all his doubts and questions were hidden in their depth. "We flirted on a couple of occasions, it's true, but it was just for fun, nothing else. There's no deeper meaning behind it. And Liv... she just needs you there by her side. That's all you need to do. You don't fix her life or Nova's, you're just their brother," she said. He was looking at the floor. She squeezed his shoulders. "Why aren't you saying anything?"

"Nothing else... This—us—is nothing else, you said. There are a million things I'd like to say to you and that you deserve to hear, but I can't. I can't." He put his forehead against hers and grabbed the back of her neck.

"I know," she replied. "I'll always be your friend. Always. I'll tease you, and you'll tease me back. I will tell you some harsh truths nobody else dares to tell you, and you won't get mad at me, at least not for long. And I'll listen to you whenever life becomes too much. I'll bring your children—and Liv's and Nova's—crazy presents from my trips, and be their weird aunt. And we'll all live our best lives. And our friendship will be beautiful and meaningful, and we'll always be there for each other." Liam lifted his head. He pressed his lips into a tight line. He was lost in thought until he seemed to come to a decision. His eyes turned hard and determined.

"I need to go now, but we'll talk later. Tomorrow. Let's talk tomorrow, okay?"

She watched him go and realized that since she arrived at the house, her eyes always followed him whenever he left a room, and even though Ava wasn't prone to lyricism or romanticism, she was honest enough with her emotions to admit she had liked him from the moment he saw his haughty self in the coffee shop, but she also knew that he wouldn't stay with her. Who did?

20 days with Ava

Ava was ordering a coffee in the place where she first met Liam. She wasn't a masochist, but she also believed in ripping off the band-aid as soon as possible. This place was only a coffee shop, and she was determined to prove it to herself. The staff remembered her immediately and greeted her by name. She was leaning on the counter, talking to them, when she spotted Phil sitting by the window. He waved at her.

"Mastermind, have a drink with me. I haven't been able to talk to you at all since we've been here."

Ava took a seat next to him. "Not my fault. You seem to appear out of nowhere just to disappear right after. If I didn't know you better, I'd say you're up to no good."

"Thankfully, you know me better. Listen, is it true what I heard about the wedding?"

"Well, I don't know what you've heard," she replied.

"Always so tight-lipped, I never taught you to gossip. Such a shame."

"You do it already for both of us. But you haven't told me

yet what you're doing here." He rubbed the back of his neck and played with his almost empty coffee cup.

"Some matters."

Ava leaned back in her chair and took a sip of coffee while she watched him. She touched a finger on her lip, thinking.

"It cannot be related to work since you have a desk job, which means it's personal. Your family has no links to this town, so not that."

Phil laughed, but he kept moving his coffee cup in circles non-stop.

"Given up yet?" he asked.

"It's not about a friend, as you have none."

"Hey, what about you?"

"OK, let me rephrase. You'd never move your ass so far from home for a friend." He put his hand on his chest, over his heart.

"You wound me." Ava laughed and suddenly stood up from her chair. She pointed at him.

"It's a woman," she said in triumph. "It's the only reason you'd make such an effort."

Phil clapped at Ava.

"Before you ask me who it is, let me tell you that I'm a gentleman and a gentleman never tells."

She scoffed but didn't press for a name.

"One day you'll experience heartbreak and you'll be more sympathetic," he said. Ava winced and tried to school her features, but not before Phil saw it. He had no problems asking for a name, which Ava diffused. Phil's face softened. "Do I need to break someone's legs, mastermind?"

"It's not as bad as that. He's a good man, just not for me."

"Yeah? I think I have a pretty good idea who you're talking about." Ava's face remained unperturbed. "Look at us, how pitiful we've become. I'm surprised you're not fighting for him. Normally nothing keeps you from what you want."

"I don't want what isn't mine."

"Ah, I see. Well —" Before Phil could continue what he was going to say, one of the coffee shop workers came over and interrupted them. Phil had ordered a sandwich, and she was bringing it over. Once she put the plate and cutlery on the table, Phil pushed it towards Ava.

"I actually need to go," Phil said. "Have it, I already paid for it." He stood up and kissed Ava on the cheek. "You'll be alright?" he asked.

"Of course," she replied. "You know me." Phil hesitated next to her chair. He leaned over and whispered.

"You might want to check on him in a couple of hours." Ava frowned, not understanding what he meant. She called after him to ask for an explanation, but he didn't stop. Ava sat back in the coffee shop chair, deep in thought. What could Phil have meant? She stood abruptly and took a few steps towards the door, as if chasing Phil, but she realized he was gone by now and opened her purse. She called him on his mobile, but he didn't pick up. A cold shiver run down her spine. What had he meant? An idea assaulted her mind. If she was right, she had to find Phil and stop him, whatever it took.

* * *

LIAM WAS in the middle of a meeting when his phone vibrated in his pocket. He ignored it and continue listening to the conversation. It vibrated again, and again, and several times more. He pursed his lips and took his phone and checked it discreetly. He had a dozen texts from Scarlett. That was unusual for her. She was rarely so insistent when he was at work. He stood up and stepped out of the conference room, apologizing to the team. "I'll be back in a minute," he said. Scarlett's messages were all the same, "I need to see you." Worried, he dialed her number, but she didn't pick up. He texted back to her asking where she was and she sent back a hotel address. He asked the team to continue the meeting without him and told his PA to handle his agenda for the next couple of hours. Liam tried calling Scarlett again with no response. He was growing more worried, and he rushed to his car.

The drive to the hotel took less than fifteen minutes. He knew where it was. He and Scarlett had dined at its restaurant before. It was high scale, one of the most expensive ones in the city. What was Scarlett doing there in the middle of the day? Liam texted Scarlett again from the lobby. "Where are you?" he typed. A reply came back immediately, "Room 215". For a moment, Liam considered that Scarlett had organized some sexy time for the two of them. He didn't feel happy at the idea of it. But she wouldn't have done it in the middle of a working day. Something was definitely wrong. He rushed into the elevator and pressed the button to the second floor.

He knocked on her door. Scarlett opened, wearing only a robe. "Liam?" she asked as she adjusted the neck of the robe to close it further. She was wearing the same perplexed expression as Liam. "What are you doing here?"

"You asked me to come," he replied.

"What? No, I—"

"Honey, who's that?" A male voice came from inside the room. Scarlett's eyes looked panicked, and she turned around. Liam put his hand on the door and opened it wider. The door moved slowly to reveal Phil in a matching robe next to a rumpled bed.

"Liam," was all Scarlett said. Liam wasn't saying anything, he just looked at Phil with a scowl on his face.

"We've met, right?" Phil said, and he walked towards Liam with his hand extended.

"Oh, God, you used my phone," Scarlett said to Phil. Phil stopped walking and looked at her. All traces of a smile had left his face, replaced by intense eyes and a hard mouth.

"You'd never leave him otherwise," he said to her.

"You had no right," she said. Scarlett turned to Liam again. "Let's talk," she told him. "Please," she added softly. Finally, Liam moved his gaze from Phil to Scarlett.

"This is a fucking joke." Liam turned to leave, only to freeze when he saw Ava in the hotel corridor. His eyes opened wide and he clenched his fists. His nostrils flared. He continued walking, his shoulder brushing past Ava, who run after him.

"Liam," she shouted after him. "Liam, wait a second. Please, just talk to me?" He didn't stop until the elevator, pressing the button to call it repeatedly.

"What is this?" Liam asked, moving his head in her direction but not looking at her.

"I—I'm sorry," she replied.

"Why are you here? Are you in on whatever that was?"

"No, of course not. I didn't know, I promise."

"And why should I believe you? This is the single most humiliating moment of my life and I turn around and find you. Why are you here? Don't tell me it's a coincidence."

"I wanted to stop it," she said.

"So you knew it was going to happen. You said you didn't know. Did you plan this?"

"No!"

"Then how did you know it was going to happen?"

"I saw Phil earlier, and he said, he—he said—it doesn't matter." He took two long steps and cornered her by the wall.

"Why would Phil talk to you about this?"

"I promise I didn't ask him to do anything like this," she said.

"Why, Ava?" he whispered.

"He didn't tell me, not specifically. He hinted—We spoke about… things, and I believe he thought I would like to know —" she replied, her voice as low as his.

"So he did this for you? For us?" He recoiled from her, his face a mask of disgust.

"That's not fair and you know it. I didn't ask for this," she replied.

"Was it fair to me?"

"Of course not," she said instantly. He leaned into her. His breath on her neck, still ragged, raised goosebumps on her skin. A sound announced the arrival of the lift, but Liam didn't move.

"Why did you have to be here, Ava?" She could feel the cold the moment he stepped away from her and left the hotel corridor. She didn't follow him.

21 days with Ava

L iv heard a faint "come in" when she knocked on Ava's door. Her friend was sitting on a chair by the window, her legs propped up on the ledge, looking out. Liv stepped around Ava's full backpack and sat on the edge of the bed.

"I'm in the mood for tacos today. Wanna come with?"

"Sure," Ava replied, although she didn't move from her position by the window.

"We can have something different if you prefer."

"No, tacos are fine." Ava still didn't leave her chair. Liv walked around the bed and sat closer to Ava. Her friend was deep in thought, her fingers brushing her lips.

"We don't need to go out at all if you're tired," Liv offered. Ava looked at her.

"Do you think that, if I had tried, one of my parents would have stayed with me?" Liv opened her mouth, but no sound came out. She really didn't know what to say. Liv had always detested Ava's parents for what they did to her, but her friend had never shown any resentment towards them. She always assumed that Ava had made peace with it. If you asked Liv, they didn't even deserve the friendly relationship they had with her. They didn't deserve any part of her.

"Did you want them to stay?" she asked in the end.

"I fight for everything, Liv, absolutely everything. If I want it, I go for it. Why didn't I fight back then? Why did I just let them leave?" Liv thought about Ava's question.

"You were so young when that happened." Ava shook her head.

"No, because I still do it. I still let go of relationships that matter to me. Why do I fight for everything except this kind of thing?"

"I don't know. Maybe you thought it's best for the other person? You always told me your parents needed the freedom they got. You always fight for yourself, but you fight even harder for the people you care about. I know, because you've done it for me." Ava looked away again, considering Liv's words. She nodded slowly. She stood abruptly and Liv jumped from the bed startled. Ava smiled—albeit a tired one—and headed outside.

"Let's go have some tacos," she said, suddenly full of her usual energy.

"You've made a decision," Liv said, reading her friend's change of attitude.

"Indeed, I have." Ava jumped down the stairs two at a time, energized at having cleared her mind. Liv, shorter than Ava, rushed to keep up. Ava stopped at the bottom of the stairs and turned to her friend. "Liv, I'm getting my company back."

"But, but," Liv said, "I thought you didn't enjoy it anymore." When Liv reached Ava on the landing, they resumed walking.

"I thought the company would be better and grow more without me. But maybe I'm wrong. Maybe it'll be better with me because I care more about it. That's why I'm not leaving it."

"I thought the sale was almost completed." Ava opened the door and signaled to Liv to go first.

"When has that stopped me?" she answered.

* * *

SCARLETT OPENED the door with bloodshot eyes and a blotchy face. Liam looked little better himself. When she saw her in that state, he couldn't help himself and opened up his arms. They had been friends and partners for years, and he was still fond of her. She rushed into his embrace and cried on his shoulder. He caressed her back in a soothing motion.

They sat down on the sofa, a bottle of whisky in front of them, and served a couple of glasses.

"I dated him before you and I started going out," she told Liam. "It wasn't even that serious, but gosh, was it passionate."

"Did you love him?" he asked, curiosity in his voice.

"At the time, I thought I did, but I'm not really sure. He's the bad boy every girl falls far once in their lives."

"Hey, I'm a bad boy too." She laughed.

"You were never a bad boy, not even during your party animal days. All the girls knew you played fair. Phil definitely doesn't play fair and back then, for some reason, I found it exciting. When I saw him again at that coffee shop… I don't really know what came over me. I don't think I love him, but I couldn't stay away from him. He came to look for me, you know? At least that's what he said. It made me feel so special, so desired."

He twirled his glass, watching the ice cubes moving and clinking against each other.

"I've been pushing you away for a long time," he said.

"You're a busy man. I always knew that about you."

"No, no, emotionally. You know I have."

"Is it Ava?" she asked.

"Was it that obvious?" She only smiled in reply. "It's not her fault," he said. "This has been happening for some time." He took a deep breath. "I didn't want to disappoint anybody."

He knew she was deep in thought because she was pouting slightly. That was her thinking face. He always found it endearing. He tugged a stray hair behind her ear.

"I think it also scared me to leave you," she said. She stood up and grabbed more ice from the freezer. She put them in a bowl and then on the table next to the whisky. "You always made me feel safe. I remember telling a friend one time that if I couldn't make it work with you, the best man I've had ever known, would I ever have a healthy relationship?" She sat down on the sofa, leaned forward, and poured another drink. "Maybe that's why when Phil appeared, I felt so drawn to him because it was a way out."

Liam took another sip of her drink and savored it.

"When did we stop talking like this? I remember that was the best thing about us. We could talk for hours."

She smiled, remembering those times together.

"Don't you sometimes feel like we're old beyond our years?"

"What do you mean?"

"When we became engaged, I sort of tried to mold myself into what I thought a good businessman wife should be. I wanted to support you, and perhaps I fell into some subconscious bias. One time I looked at myself in the mirror and I remember thinking that I looked like a 1950s wife. I freaked out so much I threw away that outfit. But that wasn't me," she stopped mid-sentence and looked at Liam. "I actually think that I don't want to get married until I'm like thirty-five. I have… an itch that I need to scratch before I marry.

Does that make sense?" It was time for him to adopt his thinking pose. She gently smoothed his furrowed brow. "You're changing too," she continued. "I can see it. You laugh more and even goof around. And I didn't bring that change."

"I'm sorry," he said.

"Why are you apologizing, silly? You did nothing wrong."

"I almost kissed her so many times," he said. "I was planning on breaking up with you yesterday." He tilted his head back and covered his face. "I'm the worst."

"I'm not one to talk."

"The wedding planner won't believe me when I tell her we're canceling another wedding," he said, and she laughed until her sides ached. She rested her head on his shoulder and he gently stroked her arm. "How did we let it get to this point?" he asked.

"Let's agree on no more apologies," she said.

"Will you be happy?" he asked.

"Only time will tell. What will you do?" And she didn't need to explain what—or who—she was referring to.

"Have you ever been in a situation that scares you so much that you don't know what to do? I fucked up, so badly. How am I going to fix this?"

"Only one way to find out."

L iam woke up on Scarlet's sofa. They had talked well into the night, drinking, and at some point, they had both fallen asleep. She was already up, even though it was barely dawn, and he offered to make some breakfast. She gently told him to stop stalling and go home.

"You're scared shitless," she said, a hint of surprise in her voice. "I don't think I've ever seen you scared before." He laughed, but there was no humor behind it.

"I feel like I've been scared every single day for the past five years." She smoothed out the wrinkles on his forehead, a familiar gesture they both found comforting. "She scares me," he said. Scarlett shook her head.

"Why do men feel scared of confident women? Come on, go." He kissed her on the cheek and left her house.

* * *

THE HOUSE WAS quiet when he opened the door. He closed it gently, trying not to wake anybody up. He dreaded coming home and talking to her, but he didn't anticipate he'd need to wait for her to wake up. That was somehow worse. How much time will he have to overthink? He could go to the office, but it was Sunday, and he also knew that if he got lost in work, he might be there for hours and lose his window of opportunity. No, he'd have to wait and hope she hadn't gone to bed too late. At least he now had time for a shower; he must stink. However, before he could put two feet on the stairs, he heard some shouting from the outside. He paused, thinking he might have heard wrong, that it was just the wind or a branch falling, but he heard a loud voice again. As he got closer to the window, he could make out what they were saying. "Liv," someone said—shouted—over and over again. He moved the curtains aside and saw Mason at their front door. He looked disheveled, his shirt half untucked and with yellow stains. One of his shoelaces was untied and seemed to have caught a small twig along the way. His hair stuck out in all directions.

"Liv!" Mason shouted again. "Liv! I need to see you. We need to talk."

Liam's surge of anger felt like a physical thing. It run up his belly to lodge in his throat. How dare that piece of trash show up his face at their house?

Liv appeared at the top of the stairs, followed by Nova, both in their pajamas. Nova's face was still showing signs of sleep, but Liv was completely awake—and terrified. Liam closed his fists and headed towards the front door. Liv saw him and rushed after him. Somehow, she made it to the door before him, and she planted herself firmly in front of it, blocking his way. She put her hands on his chest.

"Please, Liam, don't go outside," Liv implored.

"Let me out," he said.

"I'm not moving from here," she replied.

"Do you want him back? Is that what this is?" he asked. Liv winced at his tone but stood her ground.

"I don't want you getting into a fistfight with him and getting arrested. I'll deal with him." For a moment, it looked like her words hadn't registered. He didn't look at her, his eyes were fixed on the outside. With her hands still on his chest, Liv felt his chest deflate. Liam stopped pushing to get out. He then took a step away. Liv let out a breath she didn't know she had been holding.

"Let me know if you need my help," he replied, stepping further back into the house. Liv was speechless for a second. She looked at Nova, surprised he had given in so easily. Nova just shrugged her shoulders, as equally baffled as her. "You know how to deal with him, don't you?" he added. Liv lifted her chin and squared her shoulders.

"Yes, I know exactly what to do." She whispered something in Nova's ear, opened the door, and stepped out.

Mason stopped shouting as soon as he saw her and looked visibly relieved.

"Liv," he said, approaching her, "I've missed you." She put up a hand and he stopped.

"What are you doing here, Mason?"

"Babes, I've been an ass. Please, you have to forgive me. I love you." He made to approach her again, but she put up her hand again, palm facing him. "Come on, it was just a silly joke." Liv rubbed her arms. It was chilly in the morning and she was in her pajama.

"You hurt me, Mason."

"I know, babes, and I hate myself for it."

"I don't think you know. You just want me to forgive you, but you don't really understand."

"I do, I do," he replied, dropping to his knees. Liv looked unsure.

"I don't know," she said. "I don't think you understand how what you did affected me."

"How can I show it to you? I'll do anything so you come

back, babes." She thought for a moment, considering. She looked him in the eyes and said.

"Strip." He frowned, not understanding. "Strip naked right here," she said.

"What?"

"Nobody will see you. It's not even seven in the morning and the house doesn't look out the street. I want you to understand how vulnerable I felt when I saw that video."

He hesitated, looking inside the house where he knew her family was probably watching.

"What is it?" she asked. "You cannot do it?"

"Babes," he said, "I see now what you mean. I was an ass, the worst of the worst. If I could undo what I did, trust me, I'd do it."

"Strip or leave," she said, a hard edge in her voice.

In his drunken haze, Mason had been sure he could make Liv forgive him. He never expected her to react like that. Mason thought about Liv's request. He had never had trouble getting naked in front of women before. Liv had seen him naked countless times, and who else could see him from the house? He knew Liam wasn't at home or he'd have come out and beat the crap out of him. Maybe Nova, and Liv's friend, Ava. He shouldn't be bothered by being seen by them. But in this case, it felt different. He didn't feel in control. Could he do it? This was Liv, her Liv. She didn't have a mean bone in her body. She'd probably stop him and launch into his arms before his shirt was off. He unbuttoned his shirt. Mason would like to say he was being sensual about it, but he was still drunk and his balance was a bit off. He almost fell down as he took off his shoes. His shirt got caught in his head and he had to struggle to get it past his ears. Finally, he was down to his briefs. He opened up his arms.

"See? Babes, I get it."

"I said naked," she replied. He had never seen that expression on her face before. He hesitated until he finally pulled his briefs down and stood stark naked in front of her.

"Nova," she shouted towards the house. "Come out now." Mason frowned. The door opened and Nova stepped out the front door, holding her phone up. It took him a couple of seconds to understand, but he then rushed to pull his underwear up. He tripped and fell down, the briefs still halfway up.

"Stop recording," he shouted. Liv walked over to him and crouched to his level.

"And this is still nothing compared to filming someone having sex," she hissed. "Don't come near me or my family ever again."

Mason scrambled up and grabbed his trousers. Liv and Nova turned to leave, but he put a hand on her arm.

"Babes, will you delete that video? I deleted yours."

"How could I fall in love with you?" she replied and left him alone outside.

The moment the door closed, Nova stopped the video and doubled over laughing.

"That was incredible," she said. Her loud voice resonated in the entrance. Liam was looking at her sister with a half-smile and tipped his head towards her. Liv lifted her hands and showed them how they were still trembling.

"I can't believe he did it," she said.

"And they said I'm the scary one," Liam said. Liv paced up and down the entrance, trying to blow off some adrenaline.

"I'm hungry," Liv said. "Who else is hungry?"

"I'm down for anything," Nova replied. "Breakfast, tequila… I feel like I could climb the walls."

"I'll cook. You both have done enough today," Liam said.

* * *

NOVA AND LIAM were in their second serving of scrambled eggs, but after some initial mouthfuls, Liv had stopped eating. Nova and Liam were laughing at some story about when they were kids when they noticed their sister wasn't engaging. Liam tapped her on the arm and Liv came out of her trance.

"Are you feeling guilty?" Nova asked.

"No, I don't." She looked a bit surprised at her answer.

"What are you thinking about, then?" Liam asked her.

Liv grabbed her fork again and move her eggs around the plate.

"It's just that… I don't know what to do with my life right now. When the last company I worked for went busted, I said that I'd just wait until the wedding and then look for another job. I told myself I couldn't do both at the same time, but it was an excuse. The truth is that I don't know what to do with my life. I hadn't known for quite some time."

"Nobody really knows," Nova replied.

"You know. Liam knows too. Ava knows. I'm the only one that it's stuck." She stabbed a piece of egg with too much force and the fork clanked against the plate. She put the food in her mouth and chewed angrily.

"Most people will tell you I'm making the wrong deci-sion," Nova said, stealing a glance towards Liam, who had the decency to blush. "There's no rush to decide. We've got you."

Liv propped her head on her left hand and looked at Nova, thinking. Nova took a sip of her coffee and looked at Liam, who had been too quiet for a while. Liv stamped her hand on the table, bringing their attention back to her.

"That's it," she said. "As long as I can rely on you both, I won't decide anything. I have to move out."

"And go where?" Nova asked. "I mean, I'm not saying is a bad idea, but do you know where you're going?"

"I—I don't know, but I'll figure it out. I might join Ava in her travels for a while until I find out what I want to do with my life. Oh, no, she's not going traveling anymore."

Liam moved to the edge of his chair.

"She isn't?" he asked.

"No, she's going back to her hometown for a while to focus on her company."

"I thought she was selling," Nova asked.

"When is she going?" Liam added before Liv could reply.

"She's already left."

L iam stood up abruptly. His fork fell and clattered on the floor. He walked around the kitchen aisle, only to come back around again. "She had an important meeting, apparently. Her flight must be departing right now," Liv said.

"She didn't say goodbye," he finally said. He bumped into a chair and it clattered to the floor. He cursed and picked it up. Liv pushed her plate away and crossed her arms on the table.

"I was going to play dumb, big bro, but I know something happened between you two. For her to leave like that instead of confronting it head-on, well, it had to be quite a thing." Liam could feel the attention of both sisters, but he couldn't meet their eyes.

"She was there when I found Scarlett with—when I found her," he said.

"Found Scarlett where?" Nova asked.

"What do you mean, she was there?" Liv said at the same time.

"Just that. She was there. I saw Scarlett, I turned around and there was Ava. She saw everything."

"Saw what?" Nova insisted. Liam told them everything that had happened the day before. No, it had already been two days. And he hadn't talked to Ava since? He was such an ass. Nova didn't know the story. She listened to her brother with rounded eyes. Liv knew part of it, that he had broken up with Scarlett over a disagreement, but not the details. For once, she was the less sympathetic one.

"So what? I hope you don't think Ava was involved in any of that," Liv said. "I know she wasn't. She told me that she isn't talking to Phil anymore, that they had a fallout," Liv said.

"She did?"

"Yes. I had never seen Ava so upset. And I don't believe for a second that you thought she was behind all that. You know Ava is incapable of that."

"I thought Scarlett was also incapable of cheating on me and I've been proven wrong."

Liv crossed the room and pushed her brother on one shoulder, not really hurting him, just shaking him. She then took his hand, but he refused to look at her.

"Liam, you know none of this is her fault." He took his hand away and stood up. Pacing the room, he finally said.

"No, it's mine. I—I pushed Scarlett away. I don't blame anyone but me, sister. And I certainly don't blame Ava, it's just—"

"What if we try a different approach and try not to assign blame? But Ava..."

"Ava," he replied.

"Why that reaction, Liam?" He paced around the room again while Liv waited for him to speak.

"I—" he said. "She—" He suddenly grabbed his hair and messed it all up. "She drives me crazy. Every time I see her, I just feel out of control. What's up, what's down? What's wrong or right?" He stopped his pacing and looked at his sisters. "I just didn't want her, out of all people, to see me so thoroughly humiliated," he finally said.

"I knew it," Nova exclaimed in triumph.

"Oh," Liv replied. Liam sat down in between his two sisters and they all stared at the kitchen wall, at a loss for words. Finally, Liv said, "I told you she was great." He guffawed. "You know?" she said. "I've always admired you so much, I put you on a pedestal. I never thought you'd find someone that could be a match for you. Why didn't I think of her sooner?"

"She's a match for me, and a challenge, and a humility bath, and… funny, kind, smart, beautiful, strong, gentle…"

"Maybe you're the one that is not a match for her," Liv replied.

"What does that mean?" he asked.

"You know what all this means. You're the smart one in the family."

"It means… that she cannot leave."

"No, she cannot leave," Liv repeated.

"God, she cannot fucking leave," he said, leaving his sisters smiling at his running figure.

He slammed the door open with such a force that the vase in the entrance wobbled on its pedestal, only to stop dead in his tracks. Ava was standing on the other side, her hand about to press the bell.

"You're here," he said with an uncharacteristic lack of words.

"I figured you were about to do something overly dramatic and completely unpractical, like running after me when a phone call would have been way more logical and efficient," she replied. "I wanted to save us both the scene at the airport where you profess your undying love for me." He stared at her momentarily speechless until a slow smile appeared on his face. He rested one arm on the door frame and leaned forward.

"That doesn't explain why you're here. As you said, a phone call would have been enough to tell me not to come." It was her turn to smile. She took a step forward.

"How unlike me, I know. We could have crossed each other on the road and I'd had to explain to Liv why I was back. How mortifying."

"You haven't felt embarrassed a single day of your life. Imagine how much worse it would have been for me. I'd have to beg and kneel at the airport, where they drag all those filthy suitcases around. My suit would be completely ruined."

"Your suit?" she asked. "I'm going to be late to a very important meeting and I have never, ever, been late to a meeting before."

"You can blame it on a delay in your flight, but people know me around here. I'd be the talk of the town for months. I'd never live it down." They both had ended chest to chest, their faces almost touching. "And yet..." he said, "I was on my way there." He paused, searching her face for a question he hadn't asked yet. "Ava, I'm sorry..." She licked her lips and he tensed at the sight. Somehow, they got even closer together. She took a deep breath.

"Good thing I stopped you on time, then. I'll be going to my meeting now," she said as she turned to leave. He laughed, grabbed her by the arm, and turned her back to him.

"Oh, how I hate you," and he kissed her. That's how they both found out the best way to make the other shut up. It was a long time before any of them said anything else.

Epilogue

"How are you feeling?" Nova asked Liv.

"I'm scared shitless," Liv replied. They were both standing in front of Liam's offices, looking at the building. Nova turned to Liv.

"You've got this," she said with a shake of both fists in front of her. "You've been helping me with my business and with Liam's, too. Liv, you are good at it and, most importantly, you love it."

Nova was right. Liv had been trying to figure out what she wanted to do. In the past few months, she had been helping her siblings here and there, taking some courses, and doing some part-time jobs. Working with Liam side by side, at their parents' company, had been by far her favorite thing.

"But why does he have to go for a full month?"

"It just shows how much he trusts you."

Liv took a deep breath and squared her shoulders. She let go of Nova's hand and walked towards the entrance. Her heels sounded strong on the pavement.

* * *

"When are you arriving? I'll pick you up with the car," he said on the phone. Someone spoke on the other side of the line and he shook his head. "I need a specific time. Some time between tomorrow and Saturday is not good enough. I need to organize the last meetings before the holidays and I'm going to be busy." He stood by his office window, his foot tapping on the floor. He leaned a hand on the window frame. "I know that you know what time you're getting here, so just tell me."

"OK," Ava replied. Liam turned around towards the origin of her voice. Ava was standing just inside his office, her phone in her hand. The screen was still lit up from their phone call. Liam smiled. If that could be called a smile. It was more like a sunbeam, brightening the entire space. He hung up and dropped his phone on his desk, his steps becoming wider as he rushed to join her. Ava let him come to her. She loved seeing it. It was a game of theirs. She'd show up whenever he least expected just to see him run towards her. Towards her, not away from her. Ava sometimes still had trouble believing it.

He grabbed her, one hand on her waist and the other on her neck, and kissed her. The door to his office was open and his PA and some workers saw them, but he didn't care. In the past, he would have hated it. It would have made him feel like he was losing control, like he was looking weak, but that was before her. Before he learned what strength truly looks like. When they came up for air, they were alone.

"I knew you were here already," he said.

"Sure, that's why your eyes almost popped out of your sockets." He kissed her again, a light touch of their lips.

"They do that every time they look at you, they can't help it."

"Mine do that as well when they see you, but from the back. They love your butt."

"Of course they do, like everyone else. I have a very fine butt."

"Look at you, saying 'butt' at work." He laughed and held her face.

"Yeah, I've been corrupted by an evil woman. I say butt now and do all kinds of naughty things at work." Her eyes glinted.

"Shame that your schedule is so busy." He stretched one arm over her shoulders and closed the door. He then kissed her neck, his hands lost in her hair.

"My schedule is all clear. I told you," he said against her neck, "I knew you were here." She tipped her head back and moaned.

"Mmm, I just discovered that I like it when you prove me wrong. Not that it will happen often." He laughed.

"We'll see."

* * *

DEAR READER, I want to thank you for reading the love story between Liam and Ava. I hope you enjoyed it and loved them both as much as I did. I'll admit I have particularly enjoyed writing Ava. She has been based on all the women I know, taking all the strength I see and envy. I hope to one day measure up to them.

* * *

I ALSO WANT to thank my business partner, Olive, for her help with the book. She's the romantic in the Clarke duo and her recommendations definitely made the story better. I know she'll say I was missing some spice, but that's her area. I hope she continues watching the world through rainbow-colored glasses.

* * *

THANKS TO ALBERTO for all his help with Aires Publishing. He's getting us out of big trouble.

* * *

TO MONICA, thanks for the words of encouragement and those Netflix dinners.

* * *

TO DAVID, for all the support I receive from him. He gets it every time and I can always count on his honesty. I'll never know how he has the patience to listen to the same complaints over and over again.

* * *

ONE MORE TIME, thank you.

* * *

London 2022

* * *

LILY CLARKE LIVES in London in a lovely flat she can cross in one step. She has an alternate personality that writes mystery and fantasy, some of which have made it to the top 100 on Amazon. She'll probably develop a third personality soon and start writing experimental philosophy, if such a thing exists.

* * *

SHE LOVES READING, traveling, and photography—she's basic like that. She also knits her own jumpers, pretty basic ones too.

* * *

IF YOU WRITE to her on social media, she'll 100% reply to you. Search for @lilyclarkewrites on any of the main social media platforms.

* * *

* * *

ONE MORE THING.

* * *

TAKING INSPIRATION FROM AVA, I'll just say it directly: if you leave me 5 stars, you'll make me the happiest person alive. That's all I'm asking. Or at least don't give me 1 star.

Contents

1. 1 day with Ava — 1
2. 2 days with Ava — 15
3. 3 days with Ava — 23
4. 4 days with Ava — 34
5. 5 days with Ava — 39
6. 6 days with Ava — 44
7. 7 days with Ava — 50
8. 8 days with Ava — 56
9. 9 days with Ava — 65
10. 10 days with Ava — 70
11. 11 days with Ava — 75
12. 12 days with Ava — 85
13. 13 days with Ava — 101
14. 14 days with Ava — 106
15. 15 days with Ava — 120
16. 16 days with Ava — 129
17. 17 days with Ava — 133
18. 18 days with Ava — 144
19. 19 days with Ava — 152
20. 20 days with Ava — 160
21. 21 days with Ava — 166
22. 22 days with Ava — 171
23. 1 hour without Ava — 178
24. Epilogue — 182

Acknowledgments — 189
About the Author — 191
Afterword — 193

Acknowledgments

Dear reader, I want to thank you for reading the love story between Liam and Ava. I hope you enjoyed it and loved them both as much as I did. I'll admit I have particularly enjoyed writing Ava. She has been based on all the women I know, taking all the strength I see and envy. I hope to one day measure up to them.

I also want to thank my business partner, Olive, for her help with the book. She's the romantic in the Clarke duo and her recommendations definitely made the story better. I know she'll say I was missing some spice, but that's her area. I hope she continues watching the world through rainbow-colored glasses.

Thanks to Alberto for all his help with Aires Publishing. He's getting us out of big trouble.

To Monica, thanks for the words of encouragement and those Netflix dinners.

ACKNOWLEDGMENTS

To David, for all the support I receive from him. He gets it every time and I can always count on his honesty. I'll never know how he has the patience to listen to the same complaints over and over again.

One more time, thank you.

London 2022

About the Author

Lily Clarke lives in London in a lovely flat she can cross in one step. She has an alternate personality that writes mystery and fantasy, some of which have made it to the top 100 on Amazon. She'll probably develop a third personality soon and start writing experimental philosophy, if such a thing exists.

She loves reading, traveling, and photography—she's basic like that. She also knits her own jumpers, pretty basic ones too.

If you write to her on social media, she'll 100% reply to you. Search for @lilyclarkewrites on any of the main social media platforms.

One more thing.

Taking inspiration from Ava, I'll just say it directly: if you leave me 5 stars, you'll make me the happiest person alive. That's all I'm asking. Or at least don't give me 1 star.